I0661279

Max Hillary

Once for all

Vol. II

Max Hillary

Once for all
Vol. II

ISBN/EAN: 9783337053277

Printed in Europe, USA, Canada, Australia, Japan

Cover: Foto ©Andreas Hilbeck / pixelio.de

More available books at **www.hansebooks.com**

ONCE FOR ALL.

VOL. II.

LONDON:
PRINTED BY GILBERT AND RIVINGTON, LIMITED,
ST. JOHN'S SQUARE.

ONCE FOR ALL

A Novel.

BY

MAX HILLARY.

IN THREE VOLUMES.

VOL. II.

London :

SAMPSON LOW, MARSTON, SEARLE, & RIVINGTON,

CROWN BUILDINGS, 188, FLEET STREET.

1885.

ONCE FOR ALL.

CHAPTER I.

" Love requires not so much proofs, as expressions of
love. Love demands little else than the power to
feel and requite love."

Richter.

YETTA seemed to become more like
herself day by day again in all except
the gift of sight. Her mother sorrowed
for her with an acute sense—as mothers
will—of the possible disadvantage it
might be to her in the future; but her
cousin, a boy with quick feelings which
the world had not blunted, gave her more
true sympathy, and saw more of her

tears than any one else. He would lead her out upon the terrace in the evenings, when the sun, a giant which had built the proud mosque of day, was falling Samson-like, burying himself and the world in its ruins; and when the stars came out with quick eyes, like mice which play in the absence of the cat, he would tell her, in his boy's way, of the scene that was before them.

"There, you hear where the corn-crake is with his song, in which he seems to be winding up his works—well, that's the field that lies to the right of the lime-tree avenue that leads to the King's View. And all the west is yellow, and there are some blue-black clouds up above, and over the top of the trees one of the brightest of the stars shines. I wish you could see it, Yetta."

Once Yetta said to him,—

"Bernard, will you lead me up to the foot-bridge over the burn, and then up the hill-side?"

"Why do you want to go there, Yetta?"

Yetta blushed, or Bernard thought she did, but they went, and he told her where they were as they walked along; and when they came to the bridge, he said,—

"Now we are at the bridge, Yetta, but the burn is small again."

"I remember," Yetta answered; but Bernard did not know what she meant, and did not like to ask her. As they went up the hill-side, Bernard found a hat.

"Hullo, here's a hat! It must be the one Mr. Ardwell lost that—"

And he stopped suddenly, remembering that it might be painful for Yetta to recall that night.

"It isn't worth carrying now; it was only a soft slouch hat, to begin with. It is not worth while returning it to him."

"Will you give it to me, Bernard?"

"It isn't worth picking up, Yetta. But there it is. I'll carry it for you, and give it you when we get back to the house. No? Very well, there it is."

"Where are we now?" asked Yetta after a time.

"Do you remember three long-legged-looking trees? They are dark firs, and stand all alone in a little copse of under-wood, just on the very brow of the hill."

"Yes."

"Well, we are close to the trees; they are only a little way above us."

"Then we are close to the place where I had my last look of the world—or of the clouds—a crowded look. The world was forced upon my eye, and then with-drawn for ever!"

"Don't say that, Yetta. I don't believe these doctors know anything. I heard Sir John say that he had no faith in medicine or mediciners."

"They are generally right, Bernard, when they take the gloomy view."

"I don't think that's the case, Yetta. Aunt was just telling me about a cute—"

"Is that the sign for a hundredweight, Bernard?" she asked with a smile.

"No, it isn't; but I wish you would smile often like that. Well, he was very sharp or intelligent, and whenever a patient consulted him, he always shook his head, as they do when there's very little in a bottle, and that is of a good quality that jumbling won't spoil; and after shaking his head he would say, 'A desperate case.' Then if the person died, he was thought clever, because he had foreseen the result; and if the person lived, he was thought clever, because he had rescued the person from the very jaws of death. Don't you see?"

"Yes, I see. Let me stand still a little while here, Bernard."

They stood still, and he did not speak. One is almost sorry when one sees the fine material which we possess in the young, and know how little is made of it in the mature. Bernard Winn was an ordinary boy, with a quick, delicate sympathy, and much incisive power of perception. The world would change the boy's sympathy into rough prejudice in the man, and make his sharp intelligence a rude, blunt instrument, more like a hammer than a knife, with more force, but less edge.

"It was here," Yetta whispered, and she pressed her hands, which held the weather-stained hat, to her breast, and Bernard wondered whether it was the hat she pressed to her heart.

But although she showed little edges of her sorrow in her cousin's presence, and kept a brave, smiling front to the world, so that people said, "How well she bears her misfortune!" and moralized upon the buoyancy of young spirits, no one heard her weep upon her bed at night, and no ear caught her whispers, which were uttered close to her pillow,—

"No one will love me now. No one could love a piece of incarnate night, a shadow of a woman. And I did so long for some love." She pressed her hand to her face, to feel if it was hot, and then she turned it up to heaven, as if she were

facing God, and whispered, "I did long
for his love."

No one heard these things, whispered
in the dark house, and had any prudent
matron known what the girl said in her
desolation, she would probably have
shaken her stiff, old head, and answered
her; for it is a doctrine rife amongst that
class, that young ladies must not give
love unsought, and that it is only the
avowal of the gentleman's partiality which
should discover to her the real state of her
own feelings, and then only if the gentleman is approved by her parents. But all
the doctrines in the world will not change
hearts, and it is a perennial blessing that
love "cometh where it listeth," in spite of
all the laws that are in the stiff code of
prudence. But had any one seen Yetta as
she went about during the day, as she
walked slowly and gracefully through the

rooms with her white hands stretched out, and her beautiful grave face ready to answer with a smile when she was spoken to, one would have believed with Mrs. Ramsay, " That she bore it like an angel, who thinks that everything that happens is for the best ; and not like a human being, who, ever since the Fall, has been looking on the worst side of things."

Once Yetta asked Mrs. Graham if Mr. Ardwell had not been to Faldoon.

" No, Yetta," she answered, " I'm glad to say he has not. That sort of people are sometimes very disagreeable. You can't show gratitude to them in the ordinary way by giving them money, and they seem to expect to be made friends upon the strength of having done you a favour."

" I am sure you do not understand Mr. Ardwell's character, mamma."

" Well, I don't know, Yetta. But I know that it is very awkward to have all sorts of people expecting to be regarded as intimate friends merely because they have done you some service. Not that Mr. Ardwell did any great service. Any other person in his position would have done the same."

" I don't think any one could have done the same," Yetta answered, with a vivid remembrance of his gentleness and care.

" I am not ungrateful, Yetta."

" No, aunt," put in Bernard, " but you wiped out the obligation by recommending him to put his feet into warm water and mustard before you knew what was the matter with him."

" That is not fair, Bernard. You know very well I did not recommend anything of the sort, for it was not I who saw Mrs.

Flint when she was here, but Fritz; and I only said I was sorry I had not had an opportunity of recommending it to him. As for not knowing what was the matter, it was easy to see what would be the matter, when he was walking about in the rain without his hat."

"I thought he would have called," said Yetta. "And I wanted to thank him, for I must have seemed rude to him that night. I scarcely said 'Thank you' to him; I was thinking so much about myself. He said he would come. Perhaps he is still ill."

"Oh, no, Yetta, he can't be ill," said Bernard, a second time enjoying the luxury of a laugh at his aunt's medical pretensions. "I dare say my aunt's maid knew about the mustard and warm water, and told Mrs. Flint. Mrs. Skin-

Flint would be a good name for her, if she keeps lodgings, wouldn't it?"

"I don't think he's ill, Yetta," remarked Mrs. Graham, in a tone of voice which showed that she thought herself ill-treated, and also indicated that she was too proud to take any notice of the persecution. "No, he can't be ill, or we would have been sure to hear of it. He has sent a messenger out with his compliments three or four times to ask how you were, and some of the servants would have been sure to have heard if he had been ill, for it would have become serious by this time."

"It would have become a case for 'Solomon's seal,' would it not, aunt?" Bernard laughed, still keeping his laughter *sotto voce*.

"I suppose we should have heard,"

Yetta said, and her cousin, who was seated near her, thought he heard her sigh.

Two days before the ball at Kinskerth, the Wardours came over to ask Yetta if she would not still fulfil her promise and come. Sir John came with his sisters, and used all the arguments he could think of to induce Yetta to consent.

"You are so fond of music, Miss Graham, that I am sure you would enjoy it," urged Miss Wardour.

"I used to be fond of dancing," Yetta answered.

"Do come, Yetta!" Frances said. "If you don't feel happy when you are there, you can go away when you like."

"You would be happy, Miss Graham," said Sir John, and he spoke earnestly; "you would feel the influence of the joy of the others, and that would make you glad."

" I think you must consent, Yetta," put
in Mrs. Graham, whose ear had caught the
peculiar sound of Sir John's voice, and
whose eyes had been fixed on his face as
he spoke.

" We are all in a conspiracy against
you, Miss Graham," remarked Miss
Wardour, as she put her hand upon
Yetta's as it lay in her lap. We are
going to make you happy by compul-
sion."

" I wonder you think that possible,"
said Yetta. " But I am not unhappy,
only I should not wish to be there to
make others feel less comfortable. The
presence of the decrepit is often a pain,
for it demands painful sympathy at a
time when it is not a luxury to give it. I
think I should only be a kill-joy."

" Nonsense, Yetta," said Frances; "and
for you to compare yourself with a Green-

wich pensioner is absurd. You would be an ornament to the rooms, wouldn't she ?"

"Of course she would," answered Bernard, who was appealed to, and who, by the contortions which he threw his face into, evidently meant to convey the impression that she herself would be another ornament. But the difficulty of expressing this may have excused, if the love of mischief dictated, Miss Frances Wardour's question,—

"Have you got the toothache, Mr. Winn ?"

"I hope you will consent, Miss Graham," said Sir John very gently, when the others were not listening; "I know, if you refuse, one person will be miserable during the dance."

Yetta did not understand whom he meant. Did he know her secret? Was Mr.

Ardwell to be there? Should she have an opportunity of thanking him? Some of them had spoken of music. They could not mean a brass band? She thought thus, and before the Wardours left she had agreed to go to the ball.

"Ah, Sir John!" remarked Mrs. Graham, "you have more influence with Yetta than I have."

·And when they were gone, Yetta said,—

"Mamma, I wish you would not say such things."

"What things, Yetta?"

"About Sir John's influence."

"Oh! that was only a joke. But I'm sure he's very kind, is he not, Yetta? He is a man of very high principle, and he has no hypocrisy about him. He always wishes to show himself in the worst colours; but I think he doesn't believe half of what he says about religion and that sort of thing. No, he's a great favourite of mine, Sir John, and you must confess that he is very kind."

" Yes, he is very kind," said Yetta.

CHAPTER II.

" Is this the ware ?   You wanted manly love,
  And here this man is offering his heart,
  And his hot words they do not stir your blood
  As one small whisper from another would."

The Recompense.

IT was a beautiful summer night.   Everybody remarked to everybody that it was
almost too hot for dancing, and some of
the more enthusiastic of the young people
expressed an opinion that it was cooler
dancing than standing still; and one inge-
nious youth said that when one danced,
one was being fanned by the air which
was stationary, and against which you
rushed, which came to precisely the same
thing as if you were stationary and the

air rushed against you. Everybody, while they remarked upon the highness of the temperature, gave Sir John Wardour the greatest praise for having done everything he could to make his guests happy and comfortable. The dancing was not in the house, but in a marquee which ran along the whole length of the building, and all the ground-opening windows had been removed, and so the ball-room communicated with the whole suite of apartments upon the ground floor. The tent was decorated by means of strips of coloured cloth which fell from the roof to the sides, and then down to the floor, and poles were also made the means of bearing festooned wreaths of evergreens and pendant bouquet medallions made of flowers. It was hung with hundreds of coloured lamps, and the limited vocabulary of the guests could suggest no comparison for it but "fairyland," a locality with which, from the numbers of times it was mentioned, people of that district seemed to be remarkably familiar. On either side of the windows which led from the house to the ball-room there were rhododendra and azaleas, which were covered with flowers, and these trees, transformed into bouquets, added much to the beauty of the scene.

"Oh, I wish you could see it, Yetta!" exclaimed Mrs. Graham, as they entered the room.

But Yetta had not time to answer, for she heard Sir John's voice bidding them welcome, and Miss Wardour saying, "It was so good of you to come."

"I must introduce you to Lady Lean-oaks, Miss Graham. She is doing the most important duty of giving the whole affair an air of respectability, and has only brought three of her children with her! But they will cease to give any annoyance in a short time, if my instructions are carried out to the letter."

Yetta and her mother were introduced to Lady Leanoaks, and her ladyship whispered to Sir John,—

"How beautiful she is! It is one of the saddest accidents I ever heard of."

"Where do you want to be placed, Miss Graham? I shall have to leave you for a time, as I have to shake hands with everybody—that is a preliminary to representing them in Parliament; but I shall soon come back and tell you all about it, and try to let you see the room with my eyes."

"I do not care where I sit. I should wish to be out of the way."

Sir John led Mrs. Graham and Yetta to one of the seats, and then went away.

" Oh ! there are the Maxwells," said
Mrs. Graham, thinking to interest Yetta
in the arrivals. " What a handsome girl
Miss Maxwell is ! She carries herself so
well. She has white roses and maidenhair
in her hair. I wonder where Bernard has
gone ? Oh, here he comes with Frances
Wardour."

As she spoke they came up, and Frances
kissed Yetta, much to the astonishment of
certain people who saw the performance,
and who, judging from the opinion of the
aristocracy that they had all high-bridged
noses and stiff haughty manners, remarked
that Miss Frances was not so ladylike as
Miss Wardour.

"I am so glad you have come, Yetta.
The ball would have been quite slow without you, and Bernard—I mean Mr. Winn
—wouldn't have been half jolly. But the
tent is beautiful. All hung with lanterns,

and that sort of thing. And there are no end of funny people here, for this dance, you must understand, has a political significance, as Agnes would say. Oh! she has been trying to persuade John to stand upon sanitarian principles. It's great fun to hear them argue. There's a man here that nobody knows. He's a tall man, with such a handsome face. I was going to shake hands with him, but your cousin wouldn't let me. Oh! there's Frank. I must go away; I'll come back and tell you about the Misses Blackburn—I think that's their name. They are horrid frights, and look as if they had pokers up their backs. But Agnes says they have the interest of the poor at heart."

"That is one reason for not being poor," said Bernard, but Frances had run away and caught Frank Maxwell by the arm, and after calling him by his Christian

name, had asked him how many dances he
was going to dance with her, and when he
answered, "The whole," she gave him her
card.

"Who in the world is 'B. W.,' Frances?
It's too bad."

"One—two—three—"

"Don't count, it's very rude of you. If
you don't take care, I'll only give you a
square dance."

"Oh, you might just as well; he's got
all the waltzes with the best tunes. It's
too bad."

"No, it is not. You should see how
well he dances. We have practised it
together. He taught me a new step."

"Well, won't you let me score out
some of these B. W.'s?"

"No, you had better not. If you do,
I'll never speak to you again, Frank."

"Won't you? Well, I have been

modest, and have only taken two waltzes and a set of lancers."

"Oh! there is Charlie Maxstone," said Miss Frances, and she tripped away to the handsome young man who had just entered.

"Bernard," said Yetta, after he had been describing the decorations of the room, "is Mr. Ardwell here?"

"No, he isn't, Yetta. Sir John told me he had been asked, but had refused. Are you sorry?" he asked gently.

"No, not sorry," she said, but her cousin had seen hope in her face when she asked the question, and had seen the light go out as he answered it.

"Isn't the band a good one?" he said, thinking it best to change the subject.

"Yes," she answered, "but I don't think I was listening to it. I happened to overhear a conversation about myself.

I couldn't shut my ears. I don't know who the people were. They were not unkind, if pity is not cruel."

"What did they say, Yetta?"

"Oh, they talked about my misfortune. They looked at it in a very practical way. But you must go away, I won't speak another word to you to-night. You must dance and enjoy yourself. How many dances have you got from Frances?"

"Don't tell anybody, but I have secured six."

The music was good, now that she could listen to it, and was not compelled to overhear some people talking about the sad accident that had happened to Miss Graham of Faldoon some weeks ago, which had disfigured her for life, but which would scarcely stand in the way of her marriage, she had such a fortune. Yetta had some pleasure in her surroundings; she knew that there were many people about her who were happy, she heard sweet laughs ripple and float above the tune, she heard merry conversation as the people passed by, but all that did not make her quite happy. She had almost prayed that she might meet Robert Ardwell, for she thought that somehow he had come to dislike her. She had very little reason for thinking it, but as to the hilarious every word is a joke, so to the depressed every circumstance adds to sorrow. True, he had been kind and gentle that night of the storm. He had seemed to be sorry for her. But he had promised to come to Faldoon, and he had never come. He seemed to avoid her. Perhaps he had refused Sir John's invitation because he thought she might be there.

But a ball-room is not the place for . one's own thoughts, however commanding

they may be.   Yetta had to think of other
things.

"How handsome Sir John is looking!"
whispered Mrs. Graham, who had just
returned to Yetta's side.   "Oh! he is
coming here."

"Miss Graham, I am afraid you must
find it unpleasant sitting here.   May I
lead you to some of the other rooms, where
there will be less draught?   A tent is all
very well for those who are dancing, but
strong airs from heaven or elsewhere do
creep in."

"Thank you," said Yetta.

He took her hand, and placed it on his
arm, and as they walked slowly round the
room Yetta said,—

"You are very good to think of me at
all."

"I am not a bit good in any way, Miss
Graham; I wish I were."

He spoke in a quick, earnest way.

"Take care, there is a small step. Now we are in the little morning room. Shall we stay here, or shall we go to the library? There will be fewer people there, and we will be further away from the noise. I like hubbub filtered through banks of air."

He led her up the broad stairs and into the library, which was not so brilliantly lighted as the other rooms.

"Now we are in the window, Miss Graham. Do you remember being here before? It looks out over the valley, and above, there are the quiet stars."

They were seated opposite the large window, and the music from below stole in gently and pleasantly, and sweet perfumes came from the garden beneath. Neither spoke for a little.

"I should have been sorry if you had

not come, Miss Graham. It was planned for you because I thought you would like it. I don't boast about it. It is a very little thing to do. I would do a great deal more. I mean to do more. I am going to follow your advice, and go into Parliament, and try to succeed in doing something before I fail. It is more manly to fail than not to try."

Yetta sat silent for a time, and then said,—

" Is there no one else in the room ? Are we quite alone ? "

" Yes, we are."

" Then I think we had better go down-stairs."

" No, not for an instant, Miss Graham. I wanted to be alone with you for a few moments, to tell you that I love you, and to ask you to be my wife."

" Oh, don't ! please, don't."

" Why not ? I *do* love you, more than
I love myself. My love for you has made
me love myself less. I am less selfish,
less despicable than I was. I don't want
to win you by praising myself, for anything
but my love—"

" But I am blind," said Yetta.

" I know you are, and I answer that I
love you."

" You are very good."

" No, I am not; but I love you. If you
will become my wife, I will work and make
my life less useless for your sake. I
shall have insatiable ambition for your
sake. I did not love you for your eyes,
Yetta."

He had caught hold of her hand, and
pressed it in his.

" I loved you for yourself."

Yetta had risen from her seat, and tears
ran down her cheeks.

" You want eyes, Yetta; let me be eyes
to you."

There was a pause, and yet it was not
empty. Yetta was busy with thoughts.
Had she any right to make this man, who
was so good as to love her, even as she
was, blind and useless, miserable? Had she
not longed for love, and was it not offered
her by one who spoke the earnest truth?
She felt grateful to him, and she almost
mistook gratitude for love.

" You will change your mind. It is not
a man's duty to lead a blind wife through
life. You will require some one who can
shine in the society which your ambition
will teach you to rule. You will weary
of the eyeless wife who has to be led
about, and who is saddening as a starless
night."

" I swear I shall not, Yetta. I believe
I know myself—perhaps too well, and had

begun to despise myself, and so I despised others. But I know I shall never cease to love you. I don't want a wife to be only an ornament when I have company. I want you to help me to be better in the company of angels who don't come to balls, but who trouble the waters of the soul in the silent watches. Do not say 'No,' Yetta. You do not know how miserable I would be without you."

" Thank you for being so good, but—"

" Don't say 'but,' Yetta," he said, as he put his arm round her, and drew her to him; "say 'Yes.'"

She did not say " Yes," but she did not withdraw herself, and there in the dim room, with the stars looking at them, he kissed her again and again, as she wept on his shoulder.

When they returned to the ball-room he

led her to where Mrs. Graham was seated, and Yetta said,—

"I think I should like to go home, mamma!"

So they went away, leaving Bernard at Kinskerth. When they were in the carriage, and it had moved away from the doorsteps, upon which Sir John still stood, Yetta put her arms round her mother, and laid her head on her shoulder, and wept, and said,—

"Oh, mother, Sir John has asked me to be his wife!"

"Well, my dear, why do you cry?"

"I said I would, mother."

"Well, Yetta, why should you weep? He will make a good husband, I'm sure, and I hope and trust you'll be happy."

"I don't think I shall," said Yetta.

"Nonsensé, child. The excitement has been too much for you. But I told you he was in love with you, and you wouldn't believe me. There, there, don't cry, Yetta."

But Yetta did cry bitterly.

CHAPTER III.

"All jealousy
Must still be strangled in its birth, or time
Will soon conspire to make it strong enough
To overcome the truth."

Davenant.

MRS. FLINT was weary, and, as she said,
"no wonder." The circumstances fully
accounted for her feelings of fatigue.
The crisis of Robert Ardwell's illness had
come and gone, and for three whole nights
Mrs. Flint had never been to bed. Her
tiredness may have had some effect upon
her temper. And there is a feeling in
one who has been martyrized that there
is such an excellent balance in his favour
to the good, that he may be a little lavish

of the good opinion of others! And Mrs. Flint had a consciousness of the three weeks of incessant toil, and of those three crowning nights during which she had never been in bed, which may have given her more acerbity than was her wont.

"Andrew," she said, "just go and open the door, and don't sit hulking there. It's my opinion that a' yer great orators and talkers are gude for nae wark. Do ye hear, Andrew? Will ye answer that door? and no keep me waiting to gang up to Mr. Ardwell's room wi' the jelly."

"Hoot! open it yersel', Betsy. Ye are as near it as I am."

"Weel, I never! Here hae I been sittin' up these three nights and toiling for these three weeks by past, and yet ye'll no sae muckle as open the door to obleege me, when I hae sae muckle to do that I dinna ken which hand to turn to!"

" But ye hae time eneugh to hear a' aboot the Kinskerth ball, although ye are unco' thrang."

" Hear to him, hear to him," answered his wife, without addressing anybody in particular, for there was no one in the kitchen whose attention she could call to what her husband was saying. " That .was four days syne, and afore Mr. Ardwell was at his warst. And as for hearin' a' aboot it, it's very little I did hear, and what I did hear wasna' very much to my likin'."

" Hoot! Mr. Ardwell might be yer ain son the way ye think aboot his welfare, and if Sir John hadna' been goin' to marry her, do ye think she would ha' married him? No' that I dislike the young man; but they folk who get up i' the warld, are as proud as Punch, and she would think she was demeaning hersel' by marrying

the like o' him, although I can mind the
time when her grandfather, auld Robert
Graham, had a small, pokin' shop in the
back street."

" There's the knock at the door again.
Will ye open it ? "

" No, I'll no' stir hand or foot."

" Weel, ye are as disobleeging as Willy
Tod, wha wouldna' gang till his father's
funeral. And as for what ye say about
Miss Graham, I dinna believe it. Wha
are they, I suld like to ken, that they suld
hold up their heads as high as their
betters? and Mr. Ardwell's a great deal
better born and bred than they are, I jalouse.
But if it's true that she is gaun to be
married till Sir John, it'll be waur for Mr.
Ardwell, for he thinks o' ougnht else but
her. She doesna' ken what's gude for
her, if she tak's Sir John in preference to
Mr. Ardwell. That's what I say."

" And didna' ye praise Sir John for a' that was good but a fortnight by past, and threap it down my throat that he was no' a tyrant, and that I was but an old fool for abusing him ? "

" Well, I hae na' changed my mind about that, and although I did say I liked Sir John, I never said I liked him better than my ain bairn upstairs."

" Hoot ! yer gaun daft ! "

" Maybe it'll be catchin' like the fever, for I hae been ower muckle wi' you, Andrew. Will ye open that door ? It's the third time the poor body's knocked. I wonder yer no' ashamed o' yersel' sitting there hand idle, and lettin' folks skin their knuckles on the door."

" Sae lang as they dinna' skin the door, I dinna' mind."

" Ye hae nae heart, Andrew Flint. To think that ye would keep me away fra' that poor young man, and him as weak as water, a' to argue wi' you aboot the opening o' a bit door, and ye see I hae a pan in my hand, or I could do it mysel' in a jiffy. There's a good man; just gang and see wha' it is. Maybe it's the gardener fra' Kinskerth. I wonder wha it can be?"

"Satisfy your curiosity, my woman. Set down the pan, and gang to the door."

"See if I'll do so much for ye as I hae done. I hae been slavin' out my life for ye, and folk have often said, 'If I were you, I wouldna' do sae much for him. Ye just spoil him.' But ye'll just feel the want o' me when I'm nailed in my coffin. And I'll tell ye what! Gin ye dinna open the door this instant, I'll no' sew the buttons on yer breeks, and then ye'll no' win to the meetin' to-night.

There ! " Mrs. Flint ended emphatically, and she felt that she was the mistress of the situation. She still had the pan in her hand, and her husband said,—

" Well, I'll open it this time, but, my woman, I'll wark ye for this."

Having given vent to this indefinite threat he went to the door, and when he opened it, he found a young gentleman standing at it, who said,—

" Well, old gentleman, you must be jolly deaf. I have been thundering here like Olympian Jove who was cloud-collecting, and I imagined I would be crowd-collecting. Do you hear that ? "

" Yes, I hear that. Ye'll be a good scholar in time, sir."

This expression of opinion, coming from a man who spoke broad Scotch, and addressed to a very successful competitor at one of the large English schools, was, in

the estimation of that young gentleman,
particularly insulting. But Bernard Winn,
for it was he, contented himself by saying,—

" Bother, you ought not to keep people
standing at the door for half an hour.
Does Mr. Ardwell live here ? "

" Yes, he does," answered Mr. Flint, and
would have felt inclined to enlarge argu-
mentatively upon the young man's expression of opinion as to the time which should
elapse between a knock and the opening
of the door, had not his wife, who had
followed him to the door after depositing
the pan upon the hob, interfered and
said,—

" Will you walk in, sir ? " and when
Bernard followed her into the kitchen she
said, " Perhaps you'll excuse the hugger-
mugger ? "

" The how-much ? " said Bernard ; but

then correcting himself he said, " Not at all," thinking that the safest expression under the circumstances.

" Ye see it's a little difficult, sir, to keep everything in order, when there's illness in the house."

" Who's ill ? " asked Bernard.

" Who's ill? Why Mr. Ardwell, the gèntleman ye cam' speerin' for. Ill ! Ill's no' the word. He's been as near death's door as ever a man was without gettin' it snecked on him. He's been ill these three weeks. Ye'll be a friend o' his ? "

" No, not exactly," said Bernard, " but I know him, and I thought it odd he should never have been out, you know ; and besides, a lady asked me to find out whether he was quite well."

This speech was made rather blunder-ingly, and it became more so as he proceeded, and he became conscious of the awkward figure he was cutting.

" Weel, if ye are no' a friend, what I was gaun to say doesna' apply to you, but I was gaun to say that they might ha' shown him some more attention. There's naebody been to see him except the doctor, and he's paid for comin', and his ain clergyman, as they ca' him, has never been near him, and it's shamfu' for a man professin' to be a minister o' the Gospel and a Christian—I can't help sayin' it."

" It is too bad," said Bernard, who felt a generous feeling towards a poor man lying three weeks ill in bed, without any one to talk to, except the scolding old lady before him—as he had suffered extremely from being compelled to lie in bed for a single day.

" It is indeed, sir, very true, and not

one of his relations ever thought it worth
their while to write and inquire why he
didna' write to them, except ane, an' she
was some cousin o' his."

"If I had known," said Bernard, "I
should have come and sat with him."

"It's very good o' you to say so. But
it wouldna' ha' done him much good, for
he's been talkin' nonsense most o' the
time."

"Has he been so bad as that?"

"'Deed he has," remarked Mr. Flint,
who was standing with his back to the
window, with his hands deep sunk in his
dog-eared pockets. "He's been wanderin'
this fortnight past, and Dr. Arbwith has
given him ower three or four times, but
Betsy's pulled him through. I'll say that
for her," he added, as if he still bore some
grudge about the dispute which had pre-
ceded the opening of the door, but was

compelled by his sense of truth to admit so much.

"I have only done my duty, Andrew, and I wish I could hae done a deal more, but what I don't like to see, is the desertion o' the poor young man by his friends. But I must say this, that Sir John Wardour has been very kind. He has been once or twice himsel' to inquire at the door, and has sent in fruit and things that he thought Mr. Ardwell would like."

"You don't mean to say that Sir John Wardour has been aware of Mr. Ardwell's illness, do you?"

"Indeed I do. He cam' here the third day that Mr. Ardwell was ill, and he's been here twice since, ae day, when I daresay he had eneugh to do at hame, as it was the day o' the ball at Kins-kerth—"

"That's funny," said Bernard, which

had more reference to his own thoughts
than to what Mrs. Flint was saying.

" Funny or no funny, it's a fac'."

" What has been the matter with him
then ? "

" Weel, sir, it's been the fever, but
no' the infectious kind which gangs
aboot frae ane to anither like. But it's
bad eneugh in a' conscience. I hae na'
been in my bed these three nights. No'
that I make ony merit o't. I daresay
Mr. Ardwell would ha' done as much for
me : but it just shows ye that it was nae
joke."

" But you say he's better now, don't
you ? "

" Yes, sir, he's better ; but as the doctor
says, and as a child can understan', he'll
take some careful nursing, for he's as
weak as water. As I said afore, it wud
mak' ye wae to see him ; his large brown

eyes starin' out o' his thin shilpit cheeks, and a' his bonny hair gone."

" How did he come to be taken ill ?"

" Weel, if ye ask my opeenion, I'll just tell ye. Ye'll maybe ken Miss Graham o' Faldoon ? "

" Yes, she's my cousin. I'm staying at Faldoon now."

" Dear, dear. Weel, ye'll ken better than I do that Miss Graham was struck blind by lightning, and that Mr. Ardwell found her sittin' on the hillside in the rain, and brought her hame. It's my belief that he must ha' took the fever then, for besides bein' out in the rain wi' Miss Graham, he run wi' a' his might into Inverkeith for Dr. Arbwith, and then he was out at Faldoon again in his wet clothes, and had na hat on through it a'."

" I know, he must have dropped it on

the hill, when he was leading Yetta, that's my cousin, down to the house."

"Weel, he took ill that verra' night, and it's my opeenion that if he hadna' been exposed to a' that rain and cauld, he wud ne'er ha' been ill at a'."

"Very likely not," said Bernard. "I suppose he's too ill to see me to-day, but if I stay at Faldoon for a week or so more, and I hope I shall, I'll come and see him."

"I'm sure he'll be real glad to see you, sir, when he's a wee bit stronger. And I daur say noo that he's got the turn, he'll pick up gie fast."

Bernard rose to go, and he thought it would please Mrs. Flint and her somewhat reticent husband if he shook hands with them, and he did so, and took his leave.

His meditations as he walked from Inverkeith to Faldoon may be best put in his own words. All translation is impossible.

" Oh, ho ! So Sir John has known about Robert Ardwell's illness all this time, and has never said a word about it. He isn't a man who throws away his cards. He plays a good game. I wonder what he was up to? Was Yetta spooney on Ardwell? Was their meeting on the hill that night of the thunder-storm planned ? No, she couldn't accept Sir John if that was the case. If she's anything, she's honest. She wouldn't tell Sir John she loved him, if she was really in love with Ardwell. And yet I always thought she had some feeling for him. I remember her taking that shocking bad hat. I remember her asking me at the ball if Mr. Ardwell was there. And now that I think of it, she's not so jolly as she ought to be. If I were engaged, I should be awfully

jolly, but Yetta seems as sad as she was
before, or sadder, and when Sir John came
the day after the ball, and she heard his
horse's hoofs on the gravel, she said, ' Oh,
lead me away, Bernard,' and I did lead
her away, and when she came down again,
her eyes were red, and I thought she
shuddered as he took her hand. Well, it
may be all right. I don't understand it.
But hang that old fellow who opened the
door and insulted me."

His meditations were something like the
above

CHAPTER IV.

"A man of disposition like a rock
  Solemn and stern and looking upon life
  With rigid features, yet within whose heart
  There are fine waters, cool in summer heats
  But in the winter warmer than the rest."

Kay.

THE conversation which passed between Mrs. Flint and her husband, subsequent to the departure of Bernard Winn, may throw some light upon many things. They had both earnest characters. Neither of them thought that the world was a playground, but each regarded it as a matter of stern solemnity, and a matter in which one had to choose between a most ascetic duty and a course of luxurious pleasure. All their conceptions

of life were rigid and grave. The sun-
shine did not make them merry; they
remembered that the night followed.
Increase did not make them glad; they
had a consciousness that rust was a
parasite of the most precious metals.
Yet, notwithstanding these views, they
were thoroughly practical people, and
never allowed their religious convictions
to interfere with their transactions with
their neighbours. They did, however,
stop short of Mrs. Ramsay's creed, if that
was rightly stated by Mrs. Flint, for
"she looked upon hersel' as ane o' the
chosen people, the world as the land o'
Goshen, and aye heard God's command
ringin' in her ears, 'ye maun spoil the
Egyptians!'"

They were not without some warm,
true feelings of generosity and kindness,
although the little kernel lay in a very

thick shell, which, to many peoples' efforts, might seem utterly impervious.

"Weel," said Mrs. Flint, when she returned to the kitchen, "he's a very nice young man, but he's given me a qualm."

"How's that, Betsy?"

"Well, this way, Andrew. He is, as ye heard, Miss Graham's cousin, and he's livin' at Faldoon. Did ye hear him say that? for ye maun hae been unco' deaf no' to hear a' that knockin' at the door," she added, with evident mischievous pleasure in the allusion to the victory which she had gained over her husband just before their visitor's entrance.

"Woman," remarked her husband in deep, guttural tones, and bringing down the clenched fist of one hand into the open palm of the other by way of emphasis, "Woman, ye are enough to provoke a saint. I hae a gude mind to go to the meetin' wi'out any breeks."

" Andrew, Andrew, what are ye sayin' ? Gang wi'out yer breeks! Ye wouldna' be sae indecent ? "

" Hoot awa', woman ; ye ken weel what I meant."

. " Weel, but listen. This is no' a matter for laughin' at. Ye heard the young gentleman say that he didna' know Mr. Ardwell was ill, and that he was sent by a leddy."

" Yes, I heard a' that. Betsy."

" But I'se warrant, wi' a' yer prophetic glances into the future o' the constitution, ye werena' gleg eneugh to understan' that."

" Maybe aye, and maybe no! Ye tell me your meanin', and after that I'll tell ye what I jalouse."

" Weel, did ye see how his mouth went

to whistle, although he didna' do it, when
he found out that Sir John Wardour had
kenned o' Mr. Ardwell's illness thae three
weeks? I saw it though! Well, what did
it mean?"

"What's the gude o' askin' me when ye
say I dinna ken?"

"Wha was the leddy, think ye, that
sent him to find out whether Mr. Ardwell
was ill or no'? Miss Graham, to be sure!
And why was it that Sir John never mentioned onything about the poor young
man's illness? was it no' because he was a
wee jealous o' him?"

"Maybe, Betsy. But gang on, woman,
gang on."

"Gang on! what mair is there to say,
Andrew? Do ye think ane can see a' things
wi' human e'en? What mair wud ye
hae?"

"Weel, I gang further than ye do.

Didna' Sir John tell ye no' to gang tellin'
o' Mr. Ardwell's illness, and no' to send
out some clavering lass to speer at Faldoon
how Miss Graham was ?"

"Yes, I tell't ye a' that mysel'."

"Weel, dinna' ye think that maybe the
young leddy was fonder o' young Mr.
Ardwell than she was o' Sir John? and
dinna' ye think it was maybe a' because
Mr. Ardwell ne'er cam' near her, and
because she didna' ken ought aboot him,
that when Sir John said, 'Will ye be my
lady?' she said, out of spite ye ken, 'I
will.' What think ye o' that, Betsy ?"

"I wis' it were true for Mr. Ardwell's
sake, for if ever a man loved a lassie, he
lo'es 'Yetta,' as he ca's her. It wud gar
a whinstane greet to hear him courtin'
her wi' his tearful e'en and wailin' voice.
I ance grat my e'en red wi' listening to
him, and then I kissed him on the fore-

head, and I carena' whether ye are jealous or no'."

"Hoot awa', Betsy. But what wud ye do? He's lyin' on his back, and Miss Graham's engaged to be married to Sir John, by a' accounts."

"Weel, if Miss Graham is a woman o' gumption, as I daresay she is frae what he said o' her when he was rambling, she would prefer Mr. Ardwell to Sir John, though he has a title, and is the laird o' Kinskerth; and if she has been trapped into marrying Sir John, it would be right to warn her, but maybe what we said to that young callant that was here, may open her e'en—I mean speeritually, poor lassie—to Sir John and his underhand ways."

"But do ye think she does kithe to Mr. Ardwell, Betsy?"

Mrs. Flint was pleased at having her

opinion asked in such a deferential way,
and inwardly resolved to indulge her
husband in other matters besides that of
the buttons to his meeting "breeks,"
while she answered with the sententious
assurance of a person who has had her
opinion asked,—

.   " Well, Andrew, I'll just tell ye this, that
I think ye are right for aince. Ye see
they were thegither under peculiar circumstances.   First, he gied her lessons in
music, and he stopped that because he was
gettin' to like the lassie : and if he got to
like her, what for shouldna' she like
him ? "

Mrs. Flint uttered this in such a way as
to show that she regarded that argument
as incontrovertible.   She was still busy in
stirring something which sent a rich
aroma through the kitchen, while she
continued,—

"Then agin, when she was sittin' all forlorn on the brae face, wha should come up but Mr. Ardwell, wi' his bonnie lang hair, wae's me, but it's a' gane noo, and I hae only keepit twa or three locks o't, and he led her down the hill, and then he scampered into Inverkeith for the doctor. Noo a' that would be apt to impress a lassie in a man's favour, even if he were na' sae weel-favoured as Mr. Ardwell. And then if she didna' care a bawbee for him, what for should she send that callant in to Inverkeith to speer what had become o' him, eh ?"

Andrew Flint felt the truth of all his wife's observations, and felt that it was best to induce her to counsel what he would himself advise, as in that case it was more likely to be acted upon. With this view he continued, in the same deferential way,—

" Weel, Betsy, I wouldna' say but ye
may be right.   And if ye were, what wad
ye say ought to be done ? "

" What can we do, Andrew, in the mean-
time, at ony rate ?   Ye wouldna' hae me
gang out and ask to see Miss Graham, and
tell her a' about it.   We maun wait until
Mr. Ardwell's able to fend for himsel',
and then we may tell him a' that's
happened.   But I never saw folk that
interfered without unco' gude reason,
wha got thankit for't.   Na, na, I hope
Miss Graham may hae the nouse to see
what kind o' game Sir John's playing
frae what we tauld the young gentleman
that was here, and I think she will, for, as
I said, I saw his mouth pucker itself up
as if he was gaun to whistle, and that's
aye a sign o' suspicion in a man."

There was a pause, during which Andrew
Flint was thinking that his wife's generali-

zation was somewhat too wide. But his
thoughts were brought back to the subject
by his wife adding, with one can hardly
calculate what amount of emphasis to the
square inch,—

"And I'll tell ye what, Andrew. If I
find out that Sir John has been trying to
win the lassie in that underhand way,
I'll confess that ye hae been right about
him all along. There!"

CHAPTER V.

"That we ought to do an action, is of itself a suffi-
cient and ultimate answer to the questions, *why* we
should do it?—how we are obliged to do it? The
conviction of duty implies the soundest reason,
the strongest obligation of which our nature is
susceptible."

Whewell.

"You ought really to try to be more cheerful, Yetta. Of course, it's a very great
deprivation. Everybody feels for you,
but you ought to try and bear up against
your sorrow. I think, on the whole, it's
better to be blind than deaf. Deaf people
are always more or less suspicious, but
blind people are often very pleasant."

"Then it's better for other people that
one should be blind; but I don't see how

you make it out that it's better for the person himself," said Bernard, who always took Yetta's quarrels upon himself.

This conversation took place one hot summer day, while they were seated in the pleasant morning-room at Faldoon, from the windows of which one saw the sea flashing back the broad lights which fell upon it from the open sky, and whence could also be seen the vapour-like hills of Cumberland, away to the south-east, beyond the broad level glory of the day-reflecting sea. To-day the window-panes were covered with noisy flies, which kept up a chorus of loud whispers, and here and there a gay-coated wasp might be seen; and when he was seen, the hunting-spirit in the man flashed out in Bernard Winn, and notwithstanding Yetta's entreaties, he insisted upon immolating every one. And he had been boasting of his achievements in killing more than a dozen that forenoon, just before the fragment of conversation recorded above took place.

"I do try not to show it," Yetta said meekly.

"That isn't it, Yetta. You know well 'enough I'm not complaining of your sorrow. I think it natural enough—quite natural; but then, you know, I think Sir John feels it. You have lost your eyes, my dear, but you have found a very good husband."

"Oh! aunt, I forgot to tell you, I believe his rent-roll in the county is close upon 13,000l.

"Nonsense, Bernard! that is not what I mean. I mean a kind husband, one who will try to make you happy. And if one tries, one is sure to succeed."

"Well, look here, aunt. I'll try to kill

that wasp. Here goes! No! missed him! That's a case in point, isn't it? There's another!"

Yetta was sitting on a low seat near the open window, listening to the notes of the birds in the trees and shrubs outside; she thought she could detect differences in the questions and answers, and wondered if, now that she was blind, she might not be able to find any hidden meanings in very ordinary sounds. She thought she heard love in all the birds' songs, and sighed to think that there was no love for her. She thought that to know love, one must love. She had confessed to her mother that she did not love Sir John, that she had felt grateful to him for loving her, when she thought all would loathe her, that she admired and respected him. But she added,—

"It isn't love, mother; it isn't love."

In answer to this, Mrs. Graham, who thought she had had some experience in her day, assured Yetta that this was just the kind of seed-corn love which grows up and bears fruit an hundred-fold; that it was the very foundation of a more enduring affection than that which is the product of sighs and glances and blushes and non-sense. She had, however, used a more powerful argument when she told Yetta that it was her duty to marry Sir John, after having allowed him to think she loved him.

"But I did not, mother."

"Yetta," said her mother severely, "don't say that; when you allowed him to kiss you, you allowed him to think that you loved him. At least, I should hope so; otherwise the world is altered very much since I was young. No, it's your duty, Yetta!"

If Yetta was to be swayed at all, it was by means of this argument of duty. She had made up her mind that she would not find duty easy to do, and when there arose two courses of action possible, and the one was easy and the other difficult, she inclined to the latter because she distrusted her own heart's choice, and thought that the finger-post of duty must point towards the difficult. So it was that she had been influenced. And when Sir John came to see her and sat beside her, and she sighed and wept, she excused herself by saying that she had not got used to the imprisonment yet, and begged him to forgive her. What man could refuse to forgive such faults when a beautiful face, with two beautiful tearful eyes, empty of sight, were held up close to his face, and a soft voice pleaded for pardon? Of course he forgave her, and pressed his

lips in a firm kiss close to hers. Then
Yetta heard from her cousin that Robert
Ardwell had been ill—very ill—and she
thought that after all he might love her,
and the thought was an agony. Bernard
had concealed all about Sir John's knowledge of the past from a feeling of delicacy,
and because he did not see that the com-
munication of it could do any good. So he
merely said that Mr. Ardwell had been
dangerously ill for some weeks, but was
now better. But even this made Yetta
more miserable. She began to doubt
what was her duty. She dared not have
loved a man who did not love her. And
that was why she had not refused Sir
John, because at the time she was convinced that Robert Ardwell did not love
her. But now the doubt, whether he did
love her or not, made her miserable. She
almost shuddered when Sir John put his

arm round her, and then she apologized so humbly.

These things had not escaped the notice of Mrs. Graham, and it was in consequence of these observations that she indulged in the present remonstrance. After a pause, during which Bernard had gallantly cut down a wasp on the wing with an ivory paper-knife, Mrs. Graham resumed the conversation.

"I have been thinking that a change would do you good, Yetta. You know the doctors said you should be amused. We might go to Switzerland. Of course you wouldn't care for the scenery, but the air would do you good; and the conversations with travelling-companions and people who sat next you at the table-d'hôte and that sort of thing, would do you good; and then Sir John would go with us, so that we would have no bother, and he is so very amusing, and, I dare say, knows all about the history of those castles on the Rhine. We would not require to take Murray."

" I should much rather stay at home, mamma. One goes to *see* the Continent."

" But there is the change of air, and the having somebody to talk to, Yetta."

" I would much rather have the air we have here, which is soft and scented, to the air which one gets in the railway, which is dusty and smoky, or on the steamboats, which is hot and oily. I would much rather talk with you and Bernard than with all the people we could meet. You mustn't go away for some time yet, Bernard," she said, turning to her cousin, " I should miss you very much if you went away."

Bernard stopped short, handkerchief in hand, in the midst of what would inevitably have proved an exciting chase, and said,—

"I should like to stay. I don't see the good of going back to school this half, and if the gov' would let me stay a few weeks longer, I would promise to grind four hours every day."

"I suppose it was Sir John who proposed Switzerland, mamma, was it not?"

"Yes, it was, Yetta, and very considerate it was of him, I'm sure; he is most thoughtful. He proposed to have down Dr.——, Dr.——, I forget what his name was, from London, who has a great reputation, and who has devoted himself to diseases of the eye. He proposed to have him down if it would be any satisfaction to my mind."

"He is very kind," said Yetta with a sorrowful sigh. She almost regretted that he was so kind. It made her lack of love to him the more heinous, and made it more imperatively her duty to keep her plighted promise to him.

"He is indeed!" Mrs. Graham went on, while she occupied herself in arranging skeins of wool. "There are very few men like him. He brought over all those books yesterday, just because he thought you would like them, and I heard him offering to drive you out in the pony phaeton. He's a most exemplary young man."

Mrs. Graham did not mean her last sentence to be an inference from her first, but an independent conclusion, resting upon unexpressed premises.

"He is very kind," repeated Yetta.

CHAPTER VI.

"Jars concealed are half reconciled; which if generally known, 'tis a double task to stop the breach at home and men's mouths abroad."

Fuller.

IT had been finally decided that Bernard should remain at Faldoon for another month at least, and he appeared to be keeping his promise, and to be working the four hours a day with an accuracy which was scarcely to be expected, and with a persistency which the fine weather and the beginning of the grouse shooting must have made somewhat difficult.

"I don't think I could do it," he remarked to Yetta, "if it was not for you. But I think I would do almost anything you asked me. I don't feel obstreperous under a request, as I do under a threat."

"I think, Bernard, you have some other reason for keeping your promise than that."

"I say, Yetta, it seems to me that you see a good deal better since you lost your eyes. Nothing escapes you."

They were sitting on a seat on the lawn beside a great birch-tree, the leaves of which were in a gentle ague-fit in the soft west wind, and the shadows of night were prowling about, and the bats fluttering round and round in the violet sky. It was at that hour of the day when the current of conversation runs deeper into the substance of life than it does in the gay day. When the darkness deepens and the " bore " of night flows from the east, with its high, starry crest, and all its little ripples of shadow, men's hearts come closer; they talk of real hopes and fears, instead of the shams and lies of the forum and market-place.

"Why don't you go over to Kinskerth now, Bernard?"

"Why?" said Bernard, winding and unwinding a laurel leaf round his fingers. "Why? because I am at work, Yetta."

"And you are at work because you promised. Is that it?"

"Of course; and besides, I begin to see that one must work. The chief end of man cannot be cricket and football. He must work and earn a living somehow. At least, I must. I wasn't born with a silver spoon in my mouth, or if I was, the nurse prigged it, and I've never seen it since."

"How were you convinced of the truth that work is the function of those who can't afford to be idle?"

"I don't know. But it's all deuced hard for a fellow."

"What is, Bernard?"

"Well, look here, Yetta. I know you suspect it, so there's no use telling you, but the fact is, I began to be very spoony on her, and I would have done anything for her. I don't know how it began. You used to laugh at me about my long walks, and always going over to High Cleugh, and I used to get hot, and so I dare say you know whom I went to meet. And she was always so jolly and kind, that I got to like her, and if she meant to—"

But this somewhat incoherent talk came abruptly to an end, and if Yetta could have seen him, she would have seen great blinding tears in his eyes. But the heart knows more than the eyes. Yetta caught the sound of the last words, and she put out her hand, and after touching his arm, sought his hand, and took it in hers, and stroked it gently, as if it had been a bird.

She asked no questions, but after a time Bernard continued,—

"She did make me think she cared for me. She always laughed, but that was her nature. And she did dance six times with me at the ball, and we sat out two. I never thought she had no heart. I always thought she talked about Frank Maxwell and Charlie Maxstone to tease me. For I'm sure Frank Maxwell is as ugly as sin, and Charlie Maxstone, although he's good-looking, he has no more brains than a statue, and as little spirit as a wren; and although she used to laugh, she used to show that she didn't dislike me. She would not have come to meet me, and she would not—"

But again the memory of the sweet past was too much for him, and he ceased speaking, partly because he was overcome, and partly because he suspected that Yetta would disapprove of those very caresses which bulked so large in the memory of the happy past. Memory is like a lake which, when it is not fed by new sweet waters, and is drained away by some other stream, becomes bitter, because the present does not add to it, and it lies there isolated amidst the hills and valleys of yesterdays.

"And does she not like you?" asked Yetta gently.

"She says she doesn't, and that she likes Frank Maxwell a great deal better than she does me; and she said he was ever so clever. But I hate men who live on their wits and bear gorgon faces into good society on the strength of their ability; and she says she only pretended to care for me for fun, and because women bait their hook with a boy to catch a man, and she only laughed at me."

" When was this, Bernard? "

" It was four or five days ago."

" And ever since then you have been toiling and working, and transferring pages of books to pages of your memory."

" Well, what else could I do? " Bernard asked with a very discontented voice. " A man must work, you know, and I wasn't going over there again to be laughed at and called a boy; she may keep her Frank Maxwell. And then I thought if I worked and did well at the 'Varsity, she might be sorry some day."

This thought again brought him close to tears, but he recovered himself enough to answer Yetta's next question.

" Had you been quarrelling when Frances said that? "

" Yes, but she began it."

" How ? "

" She would go on flirting with other
people. Frank Maxwell was at Kinskerth
at lunch, and stayed there the whole
afternoon. And he proposed a walk to
the Grotto, and Frances went away with
him, and left me to walk with Miss Wardour, for Sir John wouldn't go. And I
heard them laughing, and he was always
taking her hand to help her over places
which were as level as the road, and then
she slipped once on purpose, and he caught
her. And all this time Miss Wardour was
talking to me about the uselessness of
learning Latin and Greek, and the
absurdity of knowing anything about
ancient history, and insisting that it was
infinitely better to know about the battles
of Dettingen and Waterloo than about
Thermopylæ and Cannæ, because these
were the very roots of our to-day, and

that sort of thing, and I didn't care *that* about the whole of it ! "

The " that " was accompanied by a snap like the cracking of a whip, produced by the mutual efforts of the thumb and second finger of his right hand.

" So you thought it your duty to take Frances to task, did you ? And you said some very severe things, and remarked upon the abominable character of the outside of Mr. Maxwell's head, and the inside of Mr. Maxstone's, and thought it would be an improvement if they could both be ' fliped,' as the common people say. Is that it, Bernard ? "

" Well, I was angry. It wasn't fair of her, was it ? "

" And now, I suppose, you are sorry ? "

" No, I'm not sorry. I would be sorry if she was, but I won't give in. She must beg my pardon."

" And you would forgive her if she asked you to forget all about it ? "

" Y—yes."

" Will you carry a note for me to Kinskerth to-morrow ? "

" No, but I'll take it to the post-office. Who's it for ? "

· " For Frances ; I want her to come over and spend a day with me."

" Do you really, Yetta ? "

He asked this, and there was a very grateful ring in his voice as he put the question.

" Of course I do ! "

But she had scarcely finished the sentence, when she felt his arms thrown round her neck, and his lips against her cheek.

" You are an angel, Yetta ; you are, indeed. If it wasn't for one thing, I would be jealous of Sir John."

He heard a little sigh, and he wondered if, after all, Sir John was so lucky as he had thought him.

Frances Wardour came a few days after, but summer had disappeared, and had left a very inferior *locum tenens*, very much resembling a March day, in its place. A wind which had all sorts of sharp edges, a most angular wind, made a considerable noise in the woods, and whistled in all the crevices.

It was too cold to go out, and so they all remained in doors, Bernard being more absorbed than usual in laborious work. Had any one looked into the library, he would have perceived a table covered with open books, and a desk upon which some papers lay in business-like confusion, for hurry has an order of its own, which is at variance with the prim method of symmetry. Bernard was seated at the desk, which was drawn out from the book-covered table, and his fingers were run through his hair and supported his head, while his elbows rested on the table. A most resolute attitude! His eyes were fixed upon one of the papers before him, but he did not seem to be reading it, unless he was acquiring what may upon occasion be a useful accomplishment, the habit of reading writing upside down. Sometimes he moved from this position. Once, when there was the sound of wheels upon the gravel, he rose and ran to the window, and, sheltering himself by the window-curtain, he peered out, and had the satisfaction of seeing Frances Wardour step from the Kinskerth carriage. After that he resumed his seat, and seemed to be again in earnest about getting something into his head.

Suddenly it struck him that the paper

was upside down, and he reversed its position. Then he rose from the table, dealt two or three vigorous blows at the coal in the grate, which exorcised that good fairy, Fire, which had by that wicked genii, Nature, been imprisoned in that black rock thousands of years before, and it burst out into bright flame. Having accomplished that feat, Bernard looked at himself in the mirror which was above the mantelpiece, ran his fingers through his hair, and thought a couple of curses in connection with the names of Frank Maxwell and Charlie Maxstone. Then he took to walking up and down the room, whistling in a most defiant way, which the wind in the keyhole tried to imitate.

Meanwhile Yetta and Frances had gone to Yetta's room, and while Yetta sat on a low chair, with her busy loom-fingers weaving some wonderful edging with an ivory shuttle, Frances lay upon the sofa, with her hands behind her head, which gave her, when seen in profile, the appearance of a grasshopper. It was she who was speaking.

"It is awfully dull at Kinskerth. I do wish John would have some friends down, as he used to do at the shooting season. We used always to have a full house, but you have spoiled him, Yetta, and he has become quite ambitious, and says he won't go in for 'Joe Mantonism,' which is a phrase he has got out of some horrid atheistical book, and nothing will content him but going into Parliament, and I know it's all to please you. He talks about letting his moors, too, and some people from Manchester or Liverpool have been inquiring about them. I hope they'll take them, for they would be better than nobody."

There was a pause, and then she added quickly, turning her head to Yetta as she spoke,—

"What is your cousin doing, Yetta?"

"Working," answered Yetta, and the shuttle still shot through delicate loops, and through her pretty fingers. "Working, working. He has become quite industrious of late."

"Why is that? He used to be idle enough. He was always rambling about all over the hills when there was nothing to shoot, and now that there are grouse I wonder he doesn't go in for 'Joe Mantonism.'"

"What is Joe Mantonism?"

"Why, Joe Manton made guns, that's all I know. But is Mr. Winn going up for some examination? It seems so absurd to sit indoors and work, when it is beautiful weather outside. Don't you think so?"

"No, not altogether; unless one works, the beautiful weather will not be beautiful weather."

"That is one of your unfathomable sayings which I cannot understand, any more than 'eggs is eggs!' That is what your cousin says. I think it must be a kind of Platonic swearing."

"What is Platonic swearing?"

"You know what Platonic love is. A kind of old people's love. More like moonshine than sunlight. A kind of kiss in a mirror. Well, I call Platonic blasphemy anything that is swearing, and isn't naughty. But I wish Mr. Winn wouldn't be so disagreeable."

"What has he been doing?"

"He was very rude to me," answered Frances with a pout.

"He is generally a very gentlemanly boy, and I dare say he is sorry if he was rude," said Yetta.

"Oh! do you think so?" Frances exclaimed, as she looked at Yetta. Then rising up, she pushed a stool close to Yetta's knee and sat down upon it, and put her arms round Yetta's waist, interfering with the pretty weaving. Then she said,—

"Yetta, I'll tell you all about it. You are to be my sister, you know; so I'll confide in you—I never could in Agnes, for she has such absurd notions, and is so stuck up with all the starch that is to be abstracted from social questions, and that sort of thing. But I don't mind telling you, for you won't be angry, even if I have been wicked, will you?—and you are so good and kind. Yetta, I'm very miserable."

Yetta gave up her tatting and sat listening, while Frances went on,—

"Yes, I'm very miserable. I dare say you think I'm always happy, because I'm always laughing, but it isn't because I'm happy that I laugh."

" No ? " asked Yetta with a little surprise in her voice, and a delicate thread of irony woven through the sound.

" No, it's because I'm miserable," and there and then, in direct contradiction of her words, she laid her head on Yetta's lap, and began to cry.

" Then do you cry when you are merry ? " asked Yetta, half-smiling.

" No, I'm always miserable now. I only did it in fun, and he thought I was in earnest, and he scolded me, and I wouldn't stand that, and so we quarrelled, and he said he would never see me again, at least until he was an old man, and then he might be bald, or married, or something awful."

" Who do you mean, Frances ? Is it Mr. Maxwell you are talking of ? "

"No, I should think not! I hate Mr. Maxwell. He is as ugly as he is disagreeable; his eyes seem to be trying to find out the parallax of a star, from the diversity of their standpoint."

"What are you talking about, Frances?" asked Yetta, thoroughly puzzled by this astronomical allusion.

"Why, don't you understand it? He said it, and I thought it was sure to be clever. It means he squints."

"Who said it? Did Mr. Maxwell say it of himself?"

"No, of course not, Yetta; how stupid you are! Bernard said it. You won't mind my calling him Bernard, will you?"

"Oh, I understand. Bernard has been abusing Mr. Maxwell."

"Yes, and quite right too; only he had no right to say what he did to me, and of course 1 couldn't stand to hear Frank abused, so I got angry, and said he was ever so clever, and was a man, and these were two good qualities that Bernard Winn could not boast. I was very angry, and he was very rude, and now I'm very miserable. I told you I flirted with Frank Maxwell only for fun."

"And you don't care for him, Frances?"

"No, I don't care for him a bit. He may be clever, he says sharp things, but he never sees good in anybody. He dances like a toad, and squints with both his eyes."

"How horrible!" said Yetta.

"Don't laugh at me, Yetta, I am very unhappy."

"Then is it Mr. Maxstone you are devoted to?"

"No, you know very well I don't care for Charlie. He is good-looking, and I like to dance with him, for it makes other girls envious; but I couldn't love a man who seemed to have been made for the sake of his whiskers. No, I never cared for him. I do care for Bernard. Only he was so angry and cross, and I said such things, oh! such horrid things, that I'm afraid he will never speak to me again."

"Did you say that you had baited your hook with a minnow to catch a salmon ? "

"He hasn't told you about it, Yetta ? " cried Frances, almost jumping for joy, and starting up and kissing her on both cheeks. "And is he really sorry ? Well, if he is, it wasn't his fault at all; it was all my fault. I had no right to flirt, and I dare say I did slip my foot when we were in the glen on purpose. And I know I pretended to want to keep my boots clean, so as to make Frank offer me his hand at all sorts of places, and that was all very wrong, was it not, dear? And I don't think he meant to scold me till I said something rude to him. And I am very sorry, too, if he is. It was all my fault, wasn't it, Yetta?"

"I don't know," said Yetta, "but I know you oughtn't to quarrel. Shall we go down to the library, and see if he is hard at work?"

"I would like to see him at work, but I don't want him to think I am miserable; I might tell him afterwards, you know, but not at first, not until he said something."

As they were going downstairs, Frances whispered to Yetta,—

"Bernard is clever, isn't he? and if he is working hard, he may some day be a great man. I should like that. But, remember, don't say I'm sorry, for I am not, you know. He had no right to scold me."

When they entered the library, Bernard was seated at the desk, in the same attitude in which we saw him, and the opening of the door did not disturb him.

" Oh, how hard he works ! " said Frances softly to Yetta ; " he is so busy he does not know we are here."

She led Yetta to him, and he never stirred.

" He must be sulky," said Frances.

Yetta placed her hand on his shoulder, when Frances burst into a fit of silent laughter, and said,—

" Oh, Yetta, he is asleep ! "

It was so. The fatigues of the morning had been too much for Bernard, and he had yielded to the temptation of shutting his eyes, the better to think out some knotty problem, and had become somnolent in that most determined attitude.

"Is that the way he works?" asked Frances, who was disappointed to find the heroic labourer asleep on duty.

But Yetta touched Bernard again, and roused him.

He started, looked round, and saw Yetta behind him smiling, and Frances on the point of laughing, and for a moment felt angry with himself and every one else. But Yetta said,—

"Bernard, I want you to let me be a peace-maker. Here is Frances, who is quite willing to be sorry if you don't defend your conduct, who is quite willing to say that it was not right of her to flirt with Frank Maxwell, if you will confess you had no right to scold her; and Frances," she continued, turning to the girl, "Bernard is very sorry that he was so cross, and is quite willing to admit that he had no right to scold you, and yet he would say that he had some excuse. Now give me both your hands."

Each gave a hand to Yetta, and she brought them together and pressed them, and said,—

" Now you will be friends."

Neither spoke at first, as neither was willing to take the initiative, but both were anxious to be reconciled. At last Frances was going to speak, and Bernard thought she was going to cry, and the mistake settled it. He burst out,—

" I am sorry. I never meant to say what I did—"

But Frances interrupted him and said,—

" No, it was all my fault—but I won't do it again. You were quite right to scold me."

" Well," said Yetta, " now that you are friends, we had better go away, Frances; we only interrupt Bernard in his work."

"Oh, I forgot his work," said Frances, laughing. "He gets it up like the school-boy who read over his lesson before he went to bed, and found that he could say it in the morning. We must go."

"No, wait a minute," Bernard said, and Yetta waited, but as he said nothing more she left the room, and Frances followed her.

That night, before Yetta went to bed, Bernard came to her and said,—

"You are an angel, Yetta."

"Of darkness?" she asked, pointing to her eyes.

"No, of light, for you give light wherever you go. I want to thank you, but I can't—and I want to confess, because it doesn't seem fair to cheat you. You know when you came and made peace this morning, and were leaving the library, I said, 'Wait a minute'?"

" Well ? "

" Well, you know after I said that, I didn't say anything more, but I—I kissed Frances, and I thought it was mean to take advantage of your not seeing, so that is why I wanted to confess."

Yetta did not scold him, she only sighed, and they parted.

CHAPTER VII.

"The consciousness of being loved, softens the keenest pang, even at the moment of parting; yea, even the eternal farewell is robbed of half of its bitterness when uttered in accents that breathe love to the last sigh."

Addison.

As Robert Ardwell began to gain strength his thoughts were constantly engaged with the question, What should he do to make money? He had of late become most anxious to have some lucrative employment, but this very desire made him think worse of himself. What would he be the better if he was rich? he used to ask himself. Would he be able to lay his heart at her feet and say, " Besides my heart I offer you an establishment; we shall travel through life together—in a carriage; we shall help one another to bear ennui"? Then he thought, if she gave him love for love and money, would it be worth having? The excellence of being poor was that one was not loved for one's position or surroundings, but for one's self and for the very necessity of some kind heart. Still, though his whole nature was opposed to sordidness, he felt he must attain a position somehow; he felt that at least he must quit Inverkeith, else he would forget the money-bags, and offer the heart without them, and that, perhaps, in toiling for the obtainable trash, be might forget the unattainable excellence, or that a time might come when his money, without making him more precious in her eyes, might make a mutual love less ridiculous in the eyes of a clair-voyant world.

The autumn had now somewhat
advanced, and the whole world looked
ripe. The trees had fulfilled lavish
promises, and bent under mellow burdens.
The fields had clothed themselves in gold
with a rustling nap, and already the
reapers had scythe and sickle in hand.
On one of the brightest of bright autumn
days, Bernard offered to lead Yetta out, as
he had often done before, and to return
for her after a time. She had very
few luxuries, but one of her chief was
listening to the song of the birds and the
whisper of the wind. She would sit for
hours under some high leafy tree, and
drink in all the songs that Nature poured
into the golden goblet of the day; or try
to mark the shadows as they told of the
passing of the hours, by the heat which
fell with the sifted lights that mottled the
ground beneath the straggling foliage of

the tree. All her wine of joy was diluted
with bitter waters, and even at these
times, when Nature seemed to draw her
soul into its soul, when it seemed to
make her forget herself and know only
what was beautiful about her, she was
not without the consciousness of being
baffled by those eyes which were shut
against all the infinite vistas, the heaven-
sent lights, the strong, beautiful day, with
all its million revelations.

On this day, Bernard led her to a place
by the stream; it was not far from the
place where the noisy torrent was crossed
by the foot-bridge. At that place the
rocks rose steep above the stream, and
above the narrow path which lay by its
side; but the rocks had ferns and shrubs
in every crevice. And above all these
grew tall trees, with shade-scattering
branches, and about their feet grew a thick

undergrowth of birches and hazels and crooked thorns, in which the birds delighted to build their nests and sing.

Under the overhanging rock there was a seat, and it was here that Yetta would sit until Bernard had devoted himself for some hours to books, after which he would return and lead her back to the house. Her gratitude for his little services made him ashamed.

The sun scarcely looked into the glen that day, and yet it was warm and the air was soft. The water murmured below her where she sat, and she could hear the sound of wings and the quick notes of the birds. These things suggested thoughts to her, but her reverie, somehow, always came back to thoughts of the glen in darkness, and to the sound of the flooded stream, and of the heavy rain on the leaves and on the ground. And then she

drove these thoughts away, and said aloud
—for she thought that would make her
determination more real—it was a sort of
gentle oath,—" I will think about something else." Then she thought about Sir
John's words, and his resolution to do
something great for her sake, and she said,
half-aloud, " He is so good, so kind. I
have tried and tried to love him, but it
is so difficult, so hard, and yet I have
promised. I must ! "

Then she rose and said,—

" I could find my way to the foot-bridge ;
it is not far."

So with her right hand touching the
wall of rock, and sometimes brushing some
fern or flowering grass, she went slowly
along the little path.

" It is so narrow," she whispered, " and
he led me down here."

When she had gone some way, she

imagined that she must be close to the foot-bridge, and she stood with her face towards the stream and listened to its murmur. She was standing thus when she heard a footstep, and she listened, but it had ceased.

" It must have been fancy," she said. " I must not think about that night. Oh, that I could blot it out, as it blotted out all days ! "

She stood still, and again she heard footsteps, and they seemed to come nearer. Then she heard them on the foot-bridge, a little to her right, and she trembled. The glen was on the Faldoon property, and no one passed through it. Then it occurred to her that it must be Sir John Wardour, who had possibly heard at the house that she was in the glen, and had come to seek her. She sighed, and said,—

" Is that you, Sir John ? "

She waited an instant for an answer, but none came, and the footfalls no longer sounded on the bridge. At length she said again,—

" Who is there ? It is ungenerous to hide from one who cannot seek."

Then some one answered,—

" I did not mean that you should hear my footsteps. I only meant to gaze, and go away."

The words thrilled her, for it was Robert Ardwell who spoke, and she put out her hand to feel for the wall, that she might lean against it, and as she did so, she became too faint to stand, and would have fallen had not he caught her in his arms. But the moment was perilous. He was breathless with his fear, and then with his effort to save her. He was full of the despair of seeing her for the last time, full of sorrow at seeing her again in her blindness. These feelings made it perilous. Besides, he held her in his arms, and felt her heart beat under his hand. He pressed his lips to hers, and murmured,—

"My love, I love you."

She scarcely moved, but she felt as if she were at rest, and blessed. Again he kissed her, and she clung to him until she felt faint again, she was so happy. But happiness is like a point, position without magnitude. We say "we are happy," and the sentence is not finished before it is a lie.

Yetta became conscious of something else than her present peace and joy. She stood upright, and clasping her hands, said,—

"What have I done? It is not your fault, it is mine. I am wrong, very wrong. I had no right to think about you."

Robert Ardwell's face, which had glowed red an instant before, was now pale again. He had thought for a moment that life was worth the trouble; he had thought that there were rich moments which made up for the dreary barrenness of years; he had thought that the days to come might yield something more than a waste chaos of crumbled palaces of hope. And now as he stood there before this beautiful girl, he felt that even this huge towering hope was falling! He had not courage to speak, and at last Yetta said,—

"No, it was my fault; you do not know all. I dare not love you, I must not! I am so sorry."

Then his own pent-up thoughts made him speak :—

"The wrong was mine. I remembered for an instant that I was a man, and that you were a beautiful woman. I forgot that I was an organist, and you were an heiress."

She reared herself proudly up and said,—

"You do me an injustice. I would not think of that. I would not mind the world's gibes and jests at a girl's romance. You do an injustice to yourself to love any one concerning whom you could think so poorly."

"I scarcely know what I have said. I was mad, I am mad. I have been ill. I cannot command my thoughts; they command me. What could I say? I thought heaven was open, and I found it was closed. I am sorry."

Then Yetta spoke, not proudly, but with tears in her eyes,—

"If I had not done wrong, this might not have been so. But I had no right to say I love you, for I have promised to love another. I must not meet you again. I must try and try not to think of you."

" But promises which do not bind the heart are lies. Who would have you keep them? Who would wish to marry you without your love? Yetta—may I call you Yetta?—if you love me why should some promise make us miserable? I am poor, but I will toil for you. I am not of your rank, but I will rise for your sake. I will wait and love, if you will say that you will marry me. Name any condition. Though it were impossible, I feel I could compass it. Impossible is only a word for the half-hearted. I am whole-hearted, and all my heart is yours."

Yetta listened, it was so pleasant to hear his sweet voice and his bold words.

" Yetta, since I saw you last, I have been at death's door. But I have never

forgotten you. Even in my wild fever-
dreams, I was conscious of your presence.
I thought you were an angel who stood
between me and death. The dream may
have been an allegory, but all I can say is,
I love you."

There was a silence, and then Yetta
said,—

"I am so slow to do right. Perhaps
even now I ought not to listen; but I am
sorry for you. I must not say how sorry.
But if any words of mine could make you
think less of me, so that you might learn
to love me less and perhaps forget me, I
should be glad, because it is right. I am
sure it is right."

"It is not right, Yetta. The world is
mad. It places laws of prudence above
laws of love. And it has laws of reason
which over-ride the highest of all laws, the
law of the human heart."

"I do not know," said Yetta, with her face turned towards the earth, and her clasped hands hanging before her; "I know that I must not love you, and that you must not love me. It is very hard and difficult, but it is right. I have said to another, 'I think you are good, I know you love me;' she shuddered; 'I am grateful, and shall try to love you.' So what can I do? I must not be false to him to be true to my own heart. You would not have me swear with my heart to be true to you, when my word is promised to another. I wish you had a right to command me, and would tell me what to do. I should like to obey you."

"Does not love give me that right?"

"No, not when I have promised to marry another. Oh, it is all so dark, so dreary! But I shall pray to forget you, and I may succeed."

"Yetta, hear me, and then I shall go. I came to-day to look at you for the last time. I have been ill, and I wish I had died!"

"Oh no, no!"

"I do. What is the good of coming back to life to find it worse than any death? But all through that weary time I have been loving you. And when at length the fever left me, and I lay still, I thought that I dare not offer you my love until I was your equal in worldly position."

"Did you think so ill of me?"

"No, it was not of you, but I knew the world has some rules, and the wise man will conform to them. I shall raise myself, the battle will do me good. But I could not go away without seeing you. I came not to speak, because I knew I could not trust myself. But I thought I might look upon you, and then go away. I do not know how I came to speak, and say what I say again, I love you."

"I must not listen any more," said Yetta, "it only makes one's after-task the harder. I shall try to do what is right. Good-bye."

She held out her hand, and he took it in his. But he could not part thus. He put his arms round her, and covered her face with kisses, and whispered, "My darling," and then she stood alone, and she heard footsteps on the bridge, and they hurried away from her, and she stood there alone, alone—even the footsteps had died away.

When Bernard returned to the glen, he found that Yetta had deserted the seat under the rock. At first he felt afraid that she might have wandered away, and perhaps fallen, for the glen was narrow and the road was rough. He ran up the path which led to the bridge, and there, close to the end of the bridge, he found Yetta crouched on the ground with her face buried in her hands, weeping bitterly.

CHAPTER VIII.

" What ! give you up—you—loving as I do ?
  Why should I care that your indifference
  Is turn'd towards me, and your heart to him,
  And that he loves you ?   Should I pain myself
  To pleasure you two ?   Do you call that love ?"
  Old Play.

Mrs. Graham and Yetta were walking up and down the stone terrace which surrounded the house, one morning when the sun was shining brightly out of a showery heaven.   Mrs. Graham was again rebuking her daughter for her want of cheerfulness, and urging her to look on the bright side of things.

" It is unaccountable to me," said she, " why you should not care more for Sir John.   Is he not handsome ? "

" I cannot see his handsomeness."

" That is disingenuous, Yetta, for you know as well as I do that he is very good-looking."

" Well, let it be so."

" Then, is he not brave and clever ? I don't think I ever heard any one talk more eloquently than he does."

" Eloquence must be truth, just as beauty must be pure."

" You don't mean to say Sir John's a liar, Yetta ? "

" I don't mean to say anything about him; but I do mean to say that I don't love him, and never will."

For a time Mrs. Graham's feelings were of too painful a nature to allow her to speak. The truth is, she had set her heart upon her daughter's marriage with the young baronet. She would never have thought of sacrificing her daughter's feelings to what she considered her interests. Had she been asked her candid opinion as to marriages for money or position, she would have censured any such prostitution of that sacred rite. But in the case of Yetta and Sir John, she saw no possibility of applying these principles. She knew Sir John intimately, and she was convinced that he would make an exemplary husband. She thought she understood Yetta's character, and from that knowledge she thought that her daughter must inevitably become attached to the handsome young man. Everything seemed to point to such a marriage. Although the Grahams were not people of rank, Yetta was an heiress, and the properties of Faldoon and Kinskerth "marched" with one another: there seemed to be some higher power pointing out the appropriateness. Mrs.

Graham had seen distaste in Yetta, had seen that it was with resignation rather than with pleasure that she looked forward to marriage with Sir John Wardour, and yet these observations did not shake her faith. She felt confident that love would come. Having secured respect, you have got everything; devoted attachment is only a matter of time.

When, however, she heard Yetta speak as she had just done, she was surprised and shocked, and for a time these sentiments were too strong to admit of their expression. At last, however, she said,—

"My dear Yetta, I cannot say how much you pain me. You ought not to speak in such a way of your future husband. It is wrong, my dear."

There was a solemn tone of reproach in this rebuke, which Yetta perhaps did not hear. She was almost too busy with her own thoughts to catch delicate shades of expression.

"My husband? Surely he will not desire to be my husband when I tell him I don't love him! But if he does, I will keep my promise."

The last words were uttered slowly and sadly.

"Do think better of it, Yetta. I believe you were getting to love him before he went away, but he hasn't gone for long, and I daresay you will like him as much as ever when he comes back. I should not be surprised if he came back to-day."

"Oh, no! not to-day. I hope he won't return to-day," said Yetta in an alarmed tone. "What shall I do?" she added sadly.

"You ought to be very glad of his return. I daresay he has counted the hours and minutes, poor fellow!"

" So have I," said Yetta slowly.

" Well, I do not know what the world is coming to! and I certainly thought you would have more sense, Yetta, than to speak of his return as if it were some calamity. But if I'm not mistaken, there is Sir John!"

"'Oh, he has come back!" said Yetta, with an effort to keep all regretfulness out of her voice. " Where are we now, mamma?"

" Opposite the drawing-room windows."

" There is a seat somewhere near, is there not? I don't mean the one in the corner under the thorns, that is concealed, but one that stands on the terrace itself, and is in full view of the windows."

" Yes, there is one a little further on."

" Would you lead me to that, mamma?"

They had not to wait long before they were joined by Sir John, who had given his horse to a servant, and ran up the steps of the terrace and walked rapidly towards them.

"Well, Yetta," he said, in a pleased, happy voice, as he took both her hands and gazed into her face, "I have come back earlier almost than I dared to expect, later by the three days of absence than I hoped. Mrs. Graham," he said, turning to her, "how are you?"

"I am quite well, Sir John, and am very glad to see you back again."

Yetta felt that she ought to have said that, but she could not tell a lie. Her mother continued,—

"But I have a good deal to do, and if you will excuse me, I will leave you with Yetta."

There was a smile upon her handsome face as she said that, and then she turned and went along the terrace to the door.

"Are you glad to see me again, Yetta? Are you glad to know that I am here? If joy is at all infectious you must be, for I have not been so happy for years as I am now. It is worth while going away, when one has come back, and yet I should not wish to go away again."

He paused, and as Yetta did not speak, he said,—

"Don't let us sit here. I hate being stared at by a whole row of windows. Let us go to the seat under the thorns; may we?"

Yetta could not refuse, and he took her hand in his, and led her along the terrace.

"It is pleasanter here," he said, as he put his arm round her. "Now tell me, are you glad to see me again?"

She did not speak, so he drew her to him, and kissed her lips, but she started, and said,—

"No, no, please don't do that! I am not glad to see you again."

"Why not?" he asked, releasing her.

"I have done wrong. I must tell you all, and yet it is so difficult—so difficult."

"What is the matter, Yetta? You object to my kissing you; you say that you are sorry that I have returned, and then you burst into tears and say that something is difficult!"

Yetta made no answer, but continued to weep.

"I certainly did not expect this of you, Yetta. Other girls, I daresay, go in for such vagaries, but I always looked upon you as something far above an ordinary hysterical school-girl."

There was nothing said for a time until Yetta had dried her tears, and then she said very gently,—

"I daresay I deserve your rebuke, but what I have got to say is not easily said. I daresay you remember when you were good enough to ask me to become your wife, I did not say I loved you. At the time I felt grateful to you, and I am still, but I do not love you. I am very sorry; I have tried to do so. And if you say you wish me to fulfil my promise, if you say that it would pain you very much to lose me, I will become your wife."

She said the last words firmly, and yet there were tears in her eyes, and in her voice as she uttered them.

"But there is no one else you love, is there, Yetta?" he asked suddenly.

"I cannot say 'No,' but you shall never have cause to complain of me on that score, if you do make me your wife. I will try still, if you insist, to love you, and to forget him. If I do not succeed, it shall make no difference in my duty to you. I shall do that. It is for you to decide."

Her fingers twitched at a ribbon trimming of her dress, and her head was bent down so that he could not see her face. He took her hand, and said,—

"You may learn to love me in time, Yetta. I shall try to become love-worthy, and then it may not be so difficult. It may be selfish, but I cannot give you up. I shall try to make you happy, and I am sorry I spoke as I did just now."

It had all turned out as Yetta thought it would, and yet she seemed to have added to her misery. While the secret of her love for another was still untold, there was a vague hope that Sir John might not be contented with half a heart, and might absolve her from her promise. Now he had heard that she had no love for him, that she loved another, and still he kept

her to her promise, and her hope had
perished !

She rose from the seat, and said,—

"I think I would rather go indoors now,
please."

So he led her into the house, and she
went to her own room and shut the door.
Sir John refused Mrs. Graham's invitation
to remain at Faldoon, and after bidding
her good-bye, he began his homeward ride,
but he could scarcely guess what agonies of
grief he had left behind him.   Yetta walked
to the house so calmly, and said good-bye
and suffered his caress so quietly, that he
could scarcely have thought it was the
same woman he had parted with some
minutes before, who now lay stretched
upon her bed, her face buried in her hands,
which lay upon the pillow, her frame
shaken by sobs, her beautiful sightless
eyes red and swollen.   He would have

been surprised, and as it was, as his horse walked slowly up a hill, he thought without satisfaction upon the confession Yetta had made, and not without wonder that a man like Robert Ardwell should be preferred to himself. He knew that it was Robert Ardwell that Yetta loved, and consequently he hated him, even while he exulted in having succeeded in winning Yetta for his wife. In justice to him it must be confessed that he thought it was the best thing that could happen for Yetta Graham. He reasoned thus,—

" Of course she thinks I am selfish; she thinks that if she had been in my place she would have acted differently, would have broken off the engagement, and that sort of thing. It's all very well for a novel, but it does not do for real life. It is easy writing about generous actions, but it is difficult to do them. If she had her own way, she would be miserable. If she married the organist, she would be in no society, and I know she is fond of society, and no wonder, for she shines in it. Now I may be selfish—I am, I admit it—but I know I can love, and I do love her; I believe I could make her happy. I must get that man out of the way if I want to get the girl's love. How is it to be done?"

The answer to that important question occupied his thoughts until he reached Kinskerth, and even when he reached home he had come to no very satisfactory conclusion as to how that desirable end was to be compassed.

CHAPTER IX.

"Clocks will go as they are set ; but man,
  Irregular man's never constant, never certain."

Otway

THERE are some great questions which never will be decided, and it is possibly well that they should remain unsolved. Thus we are not yet in a position to say whether there is more happiness in anticipation, than in actual enjoyment of some great good. And it is almost equally difficult to answer, whether it is better to be constant or inconstant. When we know what is right and what is wrong, we may be able to answer the latter question, but not until then. Everybody agrees that it is best to be inconstant to a

wrong. If one has been in the belief of
an error, it is surely a praiseworthy inconstancy when he becomes conscious of
the right, and repudiates his past self in so
far as that individual belief is concerned.
So inconstancy is tolerated by many, when
the inconstancy is in the direction of a
false kind of conduct and the adoption of
a true. But some would have a race or a
man stick to his errors rather than adopt
new truths.

The question is still a moot point, and
Bernard Winn felt considerable difficulty
about it, although he really had not been
asked to solve the problem. It was not so
much with regard to head constancy that
his doubts existed, as with regard to heart
constancy. But to him the arguments
seemed identical. If it is right to wear
out and cast aside a truth, so it must be
right to wear out and cast aside a senti-

ment. If inconstancy to one's former beliefs may be an excellence, so may inconstancy to one's former affections.

After the reconciliation which Yetta had effected between himself and Frances Wardour, he was rather idle for a time. He met Frances repeatedly on High Cleugh —these were sweet meetings, but sweetness palls. Frances no longer flirted with Frank Maxwell when he went to Kinskerth to lunch, and if they did walk out and there were difficult places to be crossed, she would allow no one to help her but Bernard. All this seemed like bliss, yet Bernard was conscious that all these marks of favour did not give him the amount of happiness that he had anticipated. He sometimes felt bored when it was time to go to High Cleugh, and thought of the awful waste of time and of the long walk. When upon some of their excursions with others of the family, or friends, he found that Frances kept with him, and never paid any attention to Charley Maxstone, or to any other body, he had an acute consciousness that everybody must be laughing in their sleeves at him. He felt considerable shame at the consciousness that he did not care so much for the girl as formerly. He had felt infinite gratitude to his cousin only a few weeks back for having brought about this reconciliation, and now he almost wished that she had not succeeded. His only consolation was that this change was involuntary. He could not say by what magic it had been produced, but there, it was effected without his wish or desire. Then came the casuistical considerations, as to the excellence of inconstancy. Yetta perceived some change in him, and one day she asked him,—

"Why do you work so hard? You have not quarrelled again, have you?"

And he answered "No," curtly. He felt very much ashamed that Yetta should have seen such a change in him, and therefore he was angry.

He was in this unpleasant frame of mind when an incident occurred that modified his conduct still more. He was teaching himself to smoke, not that he particularly cared about it, he did not know or feel the sedative effects of the weed, but he was convinced that it was the right thing to do. So he was in the habit of retiring to the terrace, or the back walk through the shrubbery to the offices, after dinner, and going in for a few coughy whiffs, while he looked admiringly at the deepening colour of his meerschaum. One evening—it was a night when the sun set in unexampled glory, crimson in a crimson

sky, and when the whole landscape, as
seen through the stems of the trees in the
wood which fringed the back walk, lay in a
soft blue mist—Bernard went out as usual,
and was wandering up and down the walk
which runs from the house to the stable-
yard, and just in sight of the entrance into
the latter, when he saw some one come out
of the great gateway which leads into the
yard, and take a path which led down the
hill, through the thick and tangled wood.
This of itself would not have struck him,
for he imagined that it might be the wife
or daughter of one of the stable-men, and
he would have continued to puff, and
polish the brown bowl of his pipe upon his
sleeve, had he not seen the woman drop
something, and his obliging disposition
made him think it worth his while to go
and pick it up. He quickened his pace,
but as it was a good way from the place

where he then was to the place where the handkerchief had been dropped, he did not reach it until the woman had almost disappeared in the wood. When he did reach it, and picked it up, he saw that it was a handkerchief of fine cambric. Boys delight in mystery, and to Bernard's young imagination this handkerchief seemed to be in some way associated with possible adventure and romance. "It must have been a lady who dropped it," he reasoned, "and if so, why should a lady be going out of the stable-yard? It may have been a thief, and it may be one of Yetta's or my aunt's handkerchiefs," he thought, and then he examined the corners, but there was nothing there which enabled him to solve the mystery that the finding of the handkerchief had raised. All the while these thoughts were occurring to him, he was following as rapidly as he could the path that led through the wood, and just before he came to the place where it leaves the plantation, and runs through a sloping field, he came close upon the individual who had dropped the handkerchief.

" I beg your pardon," he said, and his words produced the effect he had antici- pated, for the person addressed stood still and turned round.

So far the effect of his words was equal to his expectation, but in other ways he was strangely surprised. The person before him was a young girl, whose face was beautiful. It was a face that a man might have loved, without considering the character that was behind it. Some faces seem beautiful because they speak of a soul. They suggest high thoughts and hopes. Such faces are half formed by nature, half by the souls which you see behind them. The face that Bernard

looked upon was not one of these. It
was simply a beautiful face, and seemed
to have no markings of soul strife. If it
had a characteristic expression, it must
have been a gentle smile. Bernard stood
there without speaking; he had no eyes for
anything but the face, he did not see
that she was plainly clad, he did not see
that she wore no gloves, that her hands
were a little coarse; he only saw her face,
and her red-brown hair, and he stood
and looked at it. She may have seen
that his admiration made him silent, for
she smiled a little smile, which made two
flower-like dimples in her cheeks, and
made her bright eyes sparkle like wine.
That recalled him to himself, and he
said,—

"I followed you to restore your handkerchief, which you dropped just before
entering the wood."

He did not like to say, "Just after leaving the stable-yard." He held out the handkerchief, and she took it from him, and he felt almost sorry her finger had not touched his.

"Thank you," she said, "I am very much obliged to you."

Her voice, Bernard thought, was as sweet as her smile, but before he could say another word, she had turned and gone away, and he was left standing there with the light of the west in his face, looking after her. He sighed as he turned to retrace his steps, and walked slowly up the path; but suddenly a thought struck him, and he quickened his pace, and so impatient did he become, that he arrived in the stable-yard out of breath from having run up the hill. He looked into the stable, but there was no one there, and going through the door which opened into the

coach-house, he found that also empty—
except of carriages. He looked into the
cow-house or "byre," and there was the
sound of munching and the pleasant smell
of the kine, but no human being. At last
he went into the harness-room, and there
he found James Milligan.

"Hulloa!" he remarked, to which the
somewhat peculiar old gentleman answered
"Hulloa!" in his own rough way.

"Well, James," said Bernard, willing to
propitiate him, "this is a fine night."

"Ou aye," answered the coachman,
still busy with a bit and a piece of
leather.

"Most of the harvest will be in by this
time, James, won't it?"

"Maybe. I haena' seen muckle o'
it mysen', forbye what was round
about."

"Is there much to lead on the farm?"

"Are ye gaun in for bein' a country gentleman, sir?"

"No, but I like to know what's going on around me."

"Doubtless, and sae do ither folk. Do ye want a handfu' o' beans? for I find that when folk come, and are unco' civil, they generally want somethin', and I hae seen young gentlemen, like yoursel', that would chew beans even on, and it occupied their jaws rather harmlessly."

"No," said Bernard, laughing, "I don't want a handful of beans, but I did come to ask you a question, James."

"There now, didna' I say there was somethin' following a' they questions about the herst and the gettin' in the corn? Man, I'll warrant ye can play carts?"

"Play how much?"

"No' play how much, but play carts—

carts—dinna' ye ken what I mean? the de'il's buke, man, and the nine o' di'monds, the curse o' Scotland, ye ken."

" Oh, cards! " said Bernard, at length understanding. " Oh, yes. I can play cards."

" Weel, weel, ca' them cards if ye like. I prefer the way I hae aye ca'ed them, and that's carts. Weel, if ye play carts, do ye keep their faces or their backs to the body ye are playin' wi' ? Aye answer me that, man."

" Oh, their backs, of course," said Bernard, getting impatient under this cross-examination.

" Weel, ye'll hae to learn that when ye want somethin' out o' folk by means o' stratagem, ye maun e'en be as carefu' to hide your purpose. Man, I saw in a jiffy that ye werena' wantin' to ken aboot the herst, and that ye speered aboot it to

get at somethin' else.   But oot wi' your
question."

James was still occupied in cleaning the
bit, and he only paused occasionally to
give the emphasis of a shrewd look to what
he was saying.   Bernard, when he had it
thus put to him, felt some difficulty in
asking the question, but he remembered
the beautiful face, and that determined
him.

"Well, it was nothing that I was
ashamed of asking," said Bernard; "it was
only this: I saw a very pretty girl go out
of the yard, a little before I came in, and
I was wondering who she was."

"What for do ye want to ken, Mr.
Winn ? "

" I have no particular reason, only she
was pretty, and I was curious to know who
she is.   I have not seen her before."

"Oh, it's just curiosity," said the old man,

diligently rubbing the curb-chain in his hand, and then he added, " And ye'll no' hae seen her afore ? "

" Oh, bother," said Bernard, who became weary of these many questions. " If you don't mean to tell me, I can find out some other way. I could follow her yet, for that matter."

" Nane o' your followin' decent lassies here, Mr. Winn, if you please," said James Milligan, with a somewhat rough-hewn dignity; " folk o' your station should keep to it, and hae nae trokings wi' their inferiors. I've seen mischief come o't more than aince, and a' the evil fa's on the lassie, and the gentleman's thought nane the waur o'. And as for your kenning wha the lassie is, I'm no' gaun to make a mystery o't. She's a bonnie lassie, and she's as good as she's bonnie. She's my o'."

" Your what ? " said Bernard.

"My o'. My grand-daughter. Dinna'
ye ken the meanin' o' that, for a' the time
ye hae been here, and a' the interest ye tak'
in what gangs on aboot you?"

"Your grand-daughter?" said Bernard,
with unfeigned astonishment in his voice.

"Yes, my grand-dochter. Do ye think
it no possible that I should hae a grand-
dochter? Or do ye think it unco' that she
should be descended frae an ill-favoured
old carlin like me?"

"No, no, I wasn't thinking that," said
Bernard politely. "But I was thinking it
was odd I had never seen her about before.
But perhaps she doesn't live here; she has
just come on a visit, is that it?"

"No, that's no' it," answered James
Milligan in rather an ill-tempered tone,
for he felt that the young man before him,
who was not ill-favoured, had no right to
be asking questions about his pretty grand-

daughter, and the little hint he had given of his experiences of ill-advised intimacies between different classes, may account for his rather unreasonable ill-temper.

" No, that's no' it, but this is it. That ever since ye hae been about Faldoon, she's been away on a visit as ye ca' it, and it was only yestere'en that she came hame. Now are ye satisfied? or is there aught mair that ye want to ken?"

" There is one thing that I want to know, and that is why Scotch servants cannot learn to be civil," said Bernard, who felt that now he had got all the information he desired he could afford to take offence at this crusty old man.

" Weel, I'll tell ye why, and that is because they hae naebody to teach them; and aye thing mair before ye gang away, Mr. Winn, there are mair important things than manners and civeelity, for ye might be

as ceevil as the de'il himsel', but wi' a' ye
wouldna' coax the keys awa' frae Peter. So
tak' a word o' advice frae an auld man, and
tak' tint to your steps, for as sure as death
there is a lake that burns wi' fire and
brimstan', and—"

But Bernard would not stay to hear the
end, but calling out "Good-night," he
walked out of the yard, not, however,
without hearing the old man call after him,
"Ye had better hae a handfu' o' beans,"
and laugh a guttural laugh to himself
as he turned and went back into the harness-room.

CHAPTER X.

" Beauty is but a vain and doubtful good,
    A shining gloss that fadeth suddenly,
  A flower that dieth when first it 'gins to bud ;
    A brittle glass that's broken presently ;
  A doubtful good, a gloss, a glass, a flower,
  Lost, faded, broken, dead within an hour."

Shakespeare.

JAMES MILLIGAN'S cottage was almost at the foot of the hill upon which Faldoon stood, and a little way off the main road to Inverkeith. It stood on the skirt of a little copse-wood, from amongst the close underwood of which some tall, solemn fir-trees rose with ruddy stems and night-like foliage up into clear air.

It was a small cottage with a thatched roof, which Nature had begun to over-thatch and beautify by great patches oi thick, green, velvet moss, and an abundant crop of house-leeks. There was a little park in which his mottled cow fed, a pig-stye built behind the cottage, and a stack of peat cut from the neighbouring bog was built up against one of the gables. There was a garden too. It was not large; indeed it was not larger than a small back green in a city, but it had many excellences. There was a thick thorn and privet hedge all round it, and in one place there was a pleasant intermixture in the hedge of a dog-rose bush and sweet briar. Then there was a little walk, boxwood edged, up the centre, and one similarly marked, cutting it at right angles in the centre. Along the sides of this walk grew some pleasant old common flowers. Close to the wicket-gate there was a bush of southernwood, or "apple ringy," and some brunette wall-flowers, interspersed here and there with an occasional yellow-blonde of the same species. Then there were some dusty-looking polyanthi, and some cowslips and the like, all pleasant to look upon, and all attracting the bees from the two hives or "skeps" which stood at the extreme end of the centre walk, crowned with ponderous sods. But it was not all for show, for there were potatoes in one of the little corners, and cabbages in another. It was a pleasant, useful little garden, and showed a good deal of careful and loving gardening.

That evening when James Milligan came down the hill, he went into the garden before entering the cottage, and walked along the little path with a softer expression in his hard, wrinkled face than it was wont to wear. It would have been difficult to predicate how any tender emotion would have expressed itself upon that gnarled front. But there it was. He looked kindly down upon some sea-pinks as if he felt for them in their deprivation of sea-breezes. He knelt down and tied up a cabbage-rose which had got detached from its stick, saying as he did so,—

"My bonny leddy, ye maun wear yer stays. Ye hae a right to haud yer head as high as the others that are in the garden up yonder, for ye hae yer charms, and I'se warrant many a bee has been preeing yer moo this day. But never let on, I'll no' tell."

He sometimes thought the flowers understood him and would say,—

"I think the man wha wud converse wi' flowers, maun hae a pure heart. Your warldly man is no' fit to understan' them.

" Shoo ! " he cried at this moment, as he rose up from tying the rose ; " Shoo ! " and he threw a stone to the place where the peas raised their long tendrils above the sticks. " Shoo ! " and at the third cry, which accompanied the fall of the stone, a blackbird, with his golden bill, flew with a querulous chirp from amongst the peas.

" What, would ye come and eat a' the marrowfats, ye greedy beasts ? I wadna' hurt ye, but ye mauna' steal."

James Milligan, however, although he did indulge in these remarks as was his wont, was not exactly himself upon that particular night. He did not spend so long in the garden that evening, but, giving a glance at the emblazoned hatch-ment of the day which was in the western sky, with a view not to any æsthetical impression, but to the ascertainment of the probable weather on the morrow, he turned and went into the cottage.

Even the commonest men pass through the most tragic events. No man, however commonplace he may be, however apathetic he may seem, but has had some of the direr experiences of life, and has shed bitter tears over calamities which are common to all, and yet none the less poignant to each.

Nobody, to look at James Milligan, would have imagined that he had met some very stern events, and had bravely combated malicious fortune. He had married early, and in the same service, in the same cottage, he and his wife had lived to see a large family around them. It was sometimes "a thought" to them how all those little ones should be fed, but they had both implicit faith in a providential government of the world, and the future was in His hands Who knows of the death of a sparrow, and can hear the hunger-cry of young ravens. But the future which was in store, was black enough. What ought to have been dawn, brought forth nothing but clouds and darkness which blotted out the light of heaven, and made the sky a pall, the world a coffin.

Three little ones died in one day. Then a year passed away, and James' Sunday mourning had been laid aside, the two ends of crape which hung from his hat behind were removed, but the sombreness of his face remained. He had a habit now of looking very grave, and when he smiled one felt that it was a plant blossoming on uncongenial soil, and that it would not live long.

But again death knocked. This time a boy some six years old was called away. The family was but three now, and in the next year the grave in the Inverkeith churchyard was opened twice, once for another child, and then for James' wife. The other two children lived.

When James told this sad story simply, and came to mention the life of these two, he used to say, " Wae's me," and then he would add in his deepest, harshest tone, " I winna' mention the boy. But the lassie was a comfort to me."

The boy had grown to be a man, and the father had been proud of him. He was strong of limb, open of countenance, and had a cheery smile. But he was too good-humoured; he fell into evil ways, so folks said, took up with men worse than himself, and soon assimilated himself to them.

A day came when the judges walked on a spring morning through the streets of Inverkeith, and John Milligan was tried that day for manslaughter, and sentenced to be transported for twenty years.

Yet James Milligan went about his work, sore-hearted, more sombre, more hard. Every one was sorry for him, yet none dared to offer him sympathy. But the one daughter that was left was, as he said, a comfort to him. She married, and lived in a cottage not far off, and it was then, when he was left alone, that he became friends with the flowers.

Some twelve years before the night of which we speak, his daughter had become a widow, and with her little girl she returned to live with her father. Black annals these! Yet who cannot number many events as terrible, many catastrophes as imperatively calling for tears and groans as these, which have been beside their own path in life.

Still James Milligan was for all a

brave man; hard, it is true, rough
indeed, rugged as a mountain. He went
on labouring, doing his honest best
through all, and still keeping the consciousness of the past with its graves,
from interfering with the cumbrous ne-
cessities of to-day.

"Well, Mary," he said, as he entered
the little kitchen and placed his rough
hand on the pretty head of his grand-
daughter. "Did ye look at the sky,
woman? Ye are aye ganging on aboot
looking for bonny things, and the sky the
night was as bonny as a peony; but I
would na' wonder if it meant rain."

"I saw the sky, grandfather. It was
beautiful."

"Well, well, I'm not saying but it's
good. If, the rainbow was a promise o'
God, why should na' such a sky as that be
a braw promise too? and if it does bring

rain, I'm no' saying that some may na want it, although I ha' had enough mysel', but ye canna expect God to hae His eye aye on my bit garden, at least no' to consider the tulips."

Mary was not prepared to enter upon such a very deep question, all she knew or cared to know was that she took pleasure in things she thought beautiful, and she thought of God whenever her heart was moved by nature's beautiful aspects.

" Where's your mother, Mary ? "

" She has gone out, but she won't be long, grandfather; she has just gone over to the cottage at the Craigfoot."

" And you are sittin' all by yersel', readin', readin'. Ye'll be far ower learned, lassie, and, as I said to ye before, I'm no' sure that muckle good 's to be got out o' books, except o' course out o' the Bible and the "Pilgrim's Progress," which,

although a human composition, is unco'
like inspiration."

"Grandfather," said Mary, "I saw a
young gentleman as I was coming down
from the yard after I had been with you.
Who would he be?"

".What was he like, Mary? There are
a wale o' young gentlemen in the warld,
ower mony, ower mony; but what was
this ane like?"

"He was not very tall, and had dark
hair, and a goodhumoured face; he must
have been about seventeen years old, I
should say, and wore a light coat."

"She kens a' aboot him, even to his
claithes," thought James.

"I suppose he is one of the Grahams,"
she continued; "but I thought there was
only the Miss Graham who got the
property, and who was struck blind in the
thunder-storm."

" He's no' ane o' the Grahams, but a
nephew o' Mrs. Graham. He's been living at the house ever sin' ye went awa,'
and he suld be at school, that's my opinion.
What do they want wi' a laddie like that
ganging aboot the place ?"

" He is good-looking, grandfather."

" Hoot, Mary. Ye ought to hae mair
sense than to gang havering about good
looks. Isn't beauty only skin-deep ? Aye,
my woman, ye may gie a keek at yersel'
in the looking-glass,"—for when her
grandfather had spoken of the depth of
beauty she had glanced at her reflection in
the little mirror over the dresser,—" but
even your ain beauty is only that deep.
What if ye had the sma'-pox and cam' oot
wi' yer face disfigured? What would ye
say then ?"

" I would rather die than that, grandfather."

" Whist, whist, Mary. Ye maunna talk like that. Mind ye, if ye were deprived o' your bonny face, and cam' out o't wi' a face as ugly as mine, it would be God's will, lass. Mind ye that, and dinna say ye would wis' yersel' dead. It's no' right."

" But good looks are everything to a woman, grandfather. Ugly men can make their way in life, but plain women can't. They have to live old maids."

" Well, Mary, that is no' sich a frightfu' thing, is't ?" asked the old man with some sense of the humour of the query. " My woman, there are waur things than no' getting a husband, as ye'll maybe find."

"I don't know," said Mary with another glance at the looking-glass.

" Ye are a light-headed lassie, Mary, that's what ye are. That reading o' books has put a lot o' nonsense in your head, and your mother spoils you, that she does."

"And so do you, grandfather," she said, as she rose up and kissed the old man.

Soon after, her mother entered the room, and Mary said,—

"We were talking about Mr. Winn, mother. Is he an Englishman?"

"Of course he is," answered James Milligan, "and I never saw an Englishman yet that was worth his parritch. I aye think o' Bannockburn when I think o' the English."

"And I think of Flodden, grandfather," said the girl with a mischievous twinkle in her eyes.

As Mrs. Gower was spreading the table for the evening meal, Mary said,—

"I want you to tell me about Miss Graham's accident, mother. You forget that I've been away for months, and you only wrote me one letter all that time. I never saw Miss Graham."

"She came here, though," said Mrs. Gower with some pride. "She came just a day or two after you left, Mary, and came in and sat down, and was quite friendly. She didn't come to pretend to give good advice, as some ladies do, or tell us how to keep a house, when they know nothing about it; but she came and talked to me just as if I had been a friend of her own. And she promised to come back, and she would have done, but one thing and another prevented her. First there was Sir John's accident—"

"Sir John's accident!" interrupted Mary eagerly. "What was that? I never heard of it."

She spoke rapidly, and then attempted to appear indifferent to the answer, without success. But neither her mother nor grandfather noticed the eagerness, as the former was cutting a loaf, and the latter had ceased to listen to the conversation, and was busy with his own thoughts while polishing the glasses of his spectacles.

" Oh, it was talked about at the time, I can tell you. Sir John one day, when he was wandering over the hills, saw two men poaching, so what did he do but run after them, and he made up and seized one of the men, and they both fell to the ground together. In the struggle a gun went off and shot Sir John in the leg, and the man got away."

" Oh ! how horrible !" cried Mary ; " but he got quite well again, mother ? "

" Oh, yes, he got well again in a week or two."

" And he's not lame, is he ? "

" No, he walks as well as ever he did."

" But what had that accident to do with Miss Graham, and her not coming to see you again ? "

" It had just this to do, Mary : that Miss Graham and her cousin, Mr. Winn, that you saw to-night, were close to Sir John when he was shot, and they had him carried down to Faldoon, and he stayed there a fortnight. I think it was a fortnight before he went back to Kinskerth, and so Miss Graham couldn't come and see the like o' me."

" Why couldn't he go back sooner, mother ? "

" Well, I don't know, Mary, about that : but I dare say it was because he had fallen in love with Miss Graham, and well he might."

" Oh ! it is impossible," said Mary almost indignantly.

" Impossible ! Why is it impossible, Mary ? "

Mary Gower could not say why she thought it impossible, but she did say,—

" Why, Miss Graham is blind, mother."

" Yes, but she wasn't blind at that time ; and as for it being impossible, I think it would be impossible for a man not to, whether she had her eyes or no, for she's as gentle as a dove, and as beautiful as an angel, isn't she, father ? "

" Ou aye, she's a' that. I hae a pleasure in driving her, but I'm not wanted now since Sir John cam' on the carpet, for he insists on driving her in the pony phaeton himsel'."

" What does it all mean, mother ? Is Miss Graham engaged to Sir John Wardour ? "

" Well, what if she is, Mary ?   I am sure it does not matter to you, does it ? "

" No," said Mary, and looked down at her hands, which were clasped in her lap, and upon one of the fingers there was a little ring.

" I believe that Sir John didn't propose to her till after she was blind—at least, so people say," went on Mrs. Gower, who was, like all her sex, who have no other means of satisfying a craving for some intellectual life, except the means of talking about other people's affairs, inordinately fond of gossip.

" But doesn't the loss of her eyes disfigure her, mother ? "

" No, not a bit; she's as beautiful as ever ; and as for her eyes, to look at them you would· say there was nothing wrong with them. They are as bright and beautiful as ever they were."

"How strange!" said Mary, as she turned the jewelled side of her ring away from her on her finger, until the ring looked like a plain marriage-ring, and then she started, and blushed, and said,—

"But you were going to tell me how Miss Graham lost her sight."

"Oh, yes. She went out for a walk, and she was, as I. have heard tell, just sitting on the hillside, looking about her, when there was a flash of lightning, and she closed her eyes, and when she opened them she could not see. Well, it was raining cats and dogs, but she just sat still, dazed maybe by the lightning, and perhaps feeling that she couldna' find her way back to the house, and she must have been sitting there for more than an hour, when Mr. Ardwell—that's the organist at the chapel at Inverkeith, a queer, eccentric creature, who gave Miss Graham lessons in music—found her sitting there, and led her down to the house, and ran away to Inverkeith for a doctor. But when the doctors came—for they sent for ane to Edinburgh, and your grandfather drove him into Inverkeith—they said that nothing could be done. And there isna' a person that knows Miss Graham that is not sorry for her."

"Then she never will recover her sight?" asked Mary, somewhat quickly.

"Everything is possible wi' God," said Mrs. Gower, who entertained the same deep religious convictions that her father did, "but in all human probability she will be blind for life."

"I can't imagine a man loving a woman who has no eyes."

"Nonsense, Mary. If Sir John loved her before, you wouldn't have him give over loving her because she couldn't see?"

"But I don't believe—isn't she very rich, mother?" the girl asked, changing her mind as to the form, if not as to the matter, of the sentence.

"Of course she is, Mary. Her uncle left her everything."

"Perhaps Sir John is not rich," said Mary, as if she was speaking to herself, and not to any one in the room.

"Rich?" said her grandfather, "yes, he's very rich. But what are riches? a prey to moth and rust, my woman, unless ye bank wi' Heaven, and that's a bank that canna break. But from a' I ken, Sir John's but a light-headed, thoughtless young man, wha thinks o' naebody but himsel', and I'm no' quite pleased wi' Miss Graham for takin' up wi' him. He's no' a gude man, for I hae heard him swear; but maist young men are tarred wi' the same stick, I'm thinking. There's that young laddie as glib wi' his aiths as a Catholic wi' his Latin ' paters.' "

" I don't think Sir John is bad," said Mary.

" What do ye ken aboot it ?　Ye dinna think evil o' any ane, and maybe it's just as weel."

" What is Miss Graham's name, mother ? "

" What is it ?　Oh, yes—Yetta."

" Yetta ?　What a funny name !　Y, E, double T, A.　I never heard the name before."

" It's some new-fangled name, I'm thinkin'," said James Milligan, with evident disgust at the adoption of any name which had not been sanctioned by custom, and become familiar by use.

" And I dare say she's very clever," said Mary, " and knows French and German, and can make lace, and paint."

"I don't know, Mary, but I should say, if she had her eyes, she could turn her hand to almost anything. But come!"

This invitation was to the evening meal. Frugal enough it was. It looked somewhat absurd to see the girl cutting her bread thinner than her mother had done, and spreading it with some daintiness. The ruby ring looked out of place in the cottage, for the table was not even covered with a cloth, the floor was not carpeted, and the walls were whitewashed.

"Tell me this," Mary said to her mother, when the old man had retired for the night, "is Miss Graham prettier than I am, mother?"

And her mother answered: "I don't think there's anybody so pretty as my Mary," and she kissed the girl, and they parted.

CHAPTER XI.

' It was Love that made men at first Poets, and ever since, whenever a man's passion for a woman begins to give him a fever in his blood, he has sought to become melodious in his utterances, with what results deafness alone does not know."

Barnes.

THE sky was full of clouds, and it looked as if the rain which James Milligan had predicted would actually fall. As Bernard Winn looked out at them from the breakfast-room window, he said to Yetta, "We have our own homespun, grey clouds to-day, Yetta, none of your gaudy Italian blue satins."

" Don't you like the blue better, Bernard?" asked Mrs. Graham, who was reading the advertisements from the Inverkeith *Courier*.

"No, I can't say I do," said Bernard, who had some particular reason for preferring a grey to a gaudy sky that day. "No, it's un-English, you know. I like Gothic architecture because you see the rafters, and know how the roof is supported; and so I like the clouds, which are the rafters of the sky. Now don't pick me up, Yetta. I know the simile is bad, it won't hold water. By the bye, how do the clouds hold water? I never can imagine how they are kept up there. I don't suppose anybody knows."

"Does it look as if it would rain?" asked Yetta, avoiding the difficult question as to the floating of the clouds.

"I think it will," said Bernard, with a twang of satisfaction in his voice.

"And you are going to Kinskerth to

luncheon, Bernard," said Mrs. Graham, looking up from her newspaper.

" No, I don't mean to go if it is wet. I said I would go if it were a fine day, but I don't want to go if it rains. I'll go and do a couple of hours' reading, and then I'll 'come and take you out for a walk, Yetta."

Having so said, he retired, and was absent two hours, during which time he was probably hard at work, although a copy of Burns was found open upon his desk in the afternoon. When he returned, although the clouds still continued to illustrate the mystery which so puzzled him, and remained aloft, he refused to think of going to Kinskerth, as he expressed his firm conviction that it was certain to rain within an hour. And when he had led Yetta out, he kept up the impression of the proximity of a shower by remarking that it would be well not to go very far away from the house. Yetta said it mattered very little to her, and so Bernard took her to the garden, and from the garden round by the way which leads back to the house by the stable-yard. It would be erroneous to say that he expected to see Mary Gower, or old Milligan's grand-daughter, as he called her to himself, upon that road; but whether he expected her or not, he did actually meet her upon that road. Mary Gower had not been satisfied with what her mother had said of her good looks, and she was anxious to see Miss Graham, that she might compare her own face with hers. So, after having written a letter, upon which some tears fell as it was being written, she looked at her-self a long time in the looking-glass, and then went out. She just posted her letter in the village post-office, and then walked back past the cottage, and kept on along the path which leads up the hill and through the wood to the stables.

When she emerged from the thick undergrowth of leafy trees, she saw Bernard Winn walking with a lady, and, as he was leading her, Mary conjectured that it must be Miss Graham. They were coming in the direction of the stable-yard from the back walk, round by the tool-house, which stands in the fir-wood behind the garden, and Mary determined to go and meet them.

When Bernard became aware that his latent hope was about to be fulfilled, he felt very guilty, and became very red, but he had, even the night before, made up his mind what to do, so he was prepared, and almost before Mary was within bowing distance, he had taken off his hat to her.

"Whom did you bow to?" asked Yetta after they had passed Mary a little way.

"A beautiful girl, Yetta. I believe she is that crabbed old coachman's granddaughter. I don't know her name, but I don't think I ever saw a prettier girl."

"And is it upon the strength of her beauty, Bernard, that you bow to her? Is there a freemasonry between all handsome people, which entitles you to acknowledge a pretty woman's presence with that' courtesy which ordinary plain people reserve for friends?"

"Don't be satirical, Yetta. I never pretended to be good-looking."

"No, I should say you were very diffident about 'your own looks, you are so anxious to give them the benefit of all the appliances of art which can make them appear to the best advantage. If you were a woman, you would paint."

" No, I wouldn't. But I do like to see a man well dressed. It is a want of respect to the people you meet, if you go about a dowdy."

" But tell me, Bernard, why did you bow to the girl ? "

"'Well, the fact is that last night I was walking along here smoking, and I saw her come out of the stable-yard, and go down the hill, and as she went she dropped her handkerchief, and I ran and picked it up, and gave it to her. And I don't see why I shouldn't bow to her. There's no harm in it."

" Did you say she was Milligan's grand-daughter ? " asked Yetta, ignoring the question as to the morality of Bernard's bow.

" Yes, so he told me."

" Then you went and asked him, Bernard ? "

"Of course I did. I wanted to know who she was."

"Well, I can tell you a good deal about her," said Yetta, "for I remember calling at James' cottage, and having a long talk with his daughter. I think her name is Gower, and she, that is the daughter, told me a very sad story about her father's life, and showed me his little garden, and told me that the old man was as fond of flowers as if they were his own children, and went and had a 'bit crack' with them after he returned home of an evening, just as if they could understand him. And ever since that time I have taken more interest in the old man, for he has had terrible sorrows, and although he has an outside like a chestnut, he has some kindly sympathy in his heart, or he would not care for flowers. It is a good sign of a man, if he loves birds and roses."

" Well, what has all this to do with his grand-daughter ? "

" Nothing, only I thought I would tell you the whole story, as it gives us something to talk about. Do you agree with me as to the excellence of the love of birds and flowers ? " she asked, with the intention of teasing him. But although Bernard would rather she had come to the part of the story that related to the heroine at once, he did not show it, for he said,—

" Oh, yes, you are always right, Yetta."

Yetta smiled, but there was a little contradictory sadness in her smile.

" Well, Mrs. Gower told me about her own daughter, who had just gone away from home on a visit to some relations, and I suppose that is the same who has just passed us."

" Well, what about her ? what is she ? "

" I don't think she is anything. But her mother said that nothing would satisfy her except becoming a governess, and that she had been sent away to a school where she got her education for almost nothing, by teaching younger children than herself. It is so like the ambition of the Scotch people."

" I thought she wasn't an ordinary country girl," said Bernard, exulting in his own perspicuity, " for when I picked up her handkerchief, I saw it was of cambric. But did you never see the girl herself? I thought she recognized you just now; as she passed she looked so hard at you."

" No, I don't think I ever saw her. What is she like ? "

" Like—like—how can I find a simile which would not insult her? She has a beautiful face, with blue eyes and red lips, and auburn hair, but I can't give you any idea of her. I tell you she is one of the prettiest girls I ever saw."

" Even that doesn't give me any very definite idea, Bernard, for I don't know what the girls you have seen are like, and I would need to be assured of your taste and appreciation being somewhat similar to my own."

" Well, but don't you know the feeling, Yetta? Haven't you felt that there are some things so beautiful, that nothing you could compare them to would convey any impression to other people who had not seen them? I think that must be a poetic feeling. Things can be described in poetry which cannot be described in prose. I don't know how, but it is a fact."

" You are not going to try to describe James' grand-daughter in verse, are you ?"

" Why not ? " He had had some thoughts of giving vent to his feelings in rhyme.

" Don't you think I could write poetry?
You give me credit for no talent."

" Oh, yes, I do, Bernard, but I think it
must be very difficult to be a poet. However, there's no harm in trying. I should
think it is better to try and do the best,
than be content with doing nothing. Will
you show me your verses ? "

" If they are good enough, and if you
will promise not to laugh at them. Ah ! I
knew it would rain," he added exultingly.
" I felt some drops on my hand. We had
better go in, Yetta."

CHAPTER XII.

" The bad passions are the schemers.   Happiness and
contentment are poor hands at a plot."

Barnes.

SIR JOHN, when he thought it would be
advantageous to get Robert Ardwell out
of the way, had no wish to do him any
harm.   On the contrary, he thought of
doing him a favour.   All he wanted, was
to gain Yetta Graham's love, as well as
her acquiescence.   This he thought might
be secured if only Mr. Ardwell was out of
the way.   The old proverb, " Out of sight,
out of mind," seemed to him to be true.
He knew that the most enduring love
could not hold out long against the frost
of absence.   Consequently he thought that

he might do his rival some kindness that would take him away from Inverkeith for a time, and which, if it came to Yetta's ears, would redound to his, Sir John's credit. He calculated on every kindly feeling in her heart turning to love in time. He was never weary of earning her gratitude by thoughtful little attentions. When he came to and went from Faldoon, he merely shook hands with her, for he knew that his forbearance would be favourably interpreted by Yetta. He used to find out all her likes and dislikes, all her desires and wishes. He was always anticipating her wishes. She scarcely knew that a thing would be agreeable to her, before she possessed it. The favour which he had made up his mind to do to Robert Ardwell, was a part of this process. One day he drove into Inverkeith in the forenoon, and had lunch at the window of the coffee-

room in the King's Arms, which overlooks
the High Street. The waiter, who stood
opposite to him, remarked that he kept
his eye upon the street almost the whole
time. After he had finished his lunch, he
went to the door and lit a cigar, and stood
there smoking until it was almost finished,
and then suddenly throwing it away he
went down the steps and walked away.
All that the waiter knew, was, that it was
about an hour before he came back.

Sir John had during lunch, and whilst
he was smoking a cigar afterwards, been
looking for Robert Ardwell; and when
he saw him come out of English Street,
and go up the High Street, Sir John went
to the former of these streets, and soon
stood before Mrs. Flint's door.

In answer to his inquiry if Mr. Ardwell
was at home, Mrs. Flint answered that he
was not, but requested Sir John to walk

in, and Sir John at once complied. " Well, how is your patient, Mrs. Flint?" he said, when he had seated himself in Mr. Flint's big wooden arm-chair beside the fire. " I have been away from home, or I would have come to see him before this."

" Well, Sir John, I'll just tell ye. Mr. Ardwell is a' right so far as his bodily health is concerned, but he's a bit queer. No' that he's daft, but he winna tak' advice, and gang to his bed at a reasonable hour, and he's workin' so hard that he'll bring on the fever again, as I was tellin' him. But it's very kind, your comin' to ask for him."

" No, I'm not so sure of that, Mrs. Flint, but I am sorry to hear he overworks himself. What does he do?"

" He's writing a book, Sir John, but it's a great secret, and naebody's to ken o't. And he sits close at it, and it's a' I

can do to get him to tak' his food, and
to gang out and get a mouthfu' o' fresh
air."

" I did not know he was literary as well
as musical."

" Weel, I think this is the first time he
ever·wrote onything, and he has some
project o' ganging awa' frae Inverkeith,
and he thinks that he wud rather be a
writer o' books than a player on the organ."

" He means to leave Inverkeith, does he ?
He will be a great loss to the people at St.
John's."

" They were my very words, Sir John.
I said, ' You'll be a loss to the folk at St.
John's, although the clergyman never
looked near ye the whole time ye were ill,'
which didna seem the conduct o' a minister o' God's Word. But he's wilfu', and
he will gang awa' wi' your leave or wi'out
your leave. And nought 'ull satisfy him,

but he maun gie up music and tak' to literature."

"Do you know why he is so anxious to go away from here?"

"Weel, Sir John, I'm no' verra gude at guessin', and of course he doesna tell me. But I'm thinkin' to mysel' that maybe some leddy has no' been sae kind to him as she ought to hae been, or maybe some fren' has played him false." Mrs. Flint thought this was a masterpiece of diplomacy. She congratulated herself upon concealing from Sir John all that he wanted to know, and at the same time giving him a rebuke which she thought he could not fail to feel. If he had imposed silence on her with reference to Mr. Ardwell's illness, with the view of making Miss Graham believe that the young man was callous to her charms and affection, and of preventing her from sympathizing with one who, if he had not risked his life in her service, had at least increased the jeopardy in which it was at the time placed, by the exposure and fatigue which he willingly undertook—he deserved rebuke. However, Sir John did not feel discomposed, and merely answered,—

"Your surmise is probably correct, but as I do not want to play him false, I want you as a friend to tell me what I could do to help him. I thought that an effort might be made to get him appointed organist in some larger church or cathedral, but if he is deserting music in favour of literature, I must try to help him in some other way."

"Will ye no' mind my speakin' my mind to ye, Sir John?"

"Not at all. You will do me a favour by telling me exactly what you think."

"Weel, I think this, that Mr. Ardwell

wouldna be very willing to accept o'
favours frae onybody, and I wouldna
wonder if he was mair stickling aboot
accepting them frae you."

" Why should that be so ? "

" I dinna ken, but when he heard that
you had been gude enough to send fruit to
him a' the time he was ill, he was gey
angry wi' me for takin' it, and wanted
to send you back what would be equi-
valent to a' he had got frae you. And
that was only the day before yesterday he
said that. And I kenna what ye could
do that he would accept, when he was
angry aboot a wheen grapes and straw-
berries. And, you see, he's going away
frae Inverkeith, and I can assure ye I'm
very sorry to lose him, for a ceeviller
young gentleman, and ane that gave less
trouble, never came within a door: but
he's promised to write a bit line now and

then to tell me how he gets on, for he aye
says he never can thank me enough for
what I did for him when he was ill—but
as for that, it was naething, naething at a'!
Although there were three nights that I
never had off my claithes."

"He would be very ungrateful indeed if
he did not feel gratitude to you, Mrs.
Flint. But when does he leave Inverkeith?"

"He speaks about goin' awa' this day
week, Sir John, and he might just as weel
be in a big toun for a' the good he gets o'
the country, sittin' day after day—for the
last three or four, at any rate—in his room,
and never liftin' his een frae his paper.
It'll be a wonder to me if he's no' ill afore
he leaves."

"Then," said Sir John, rising, "although
I cannot do anything for him, perhaps you
will allow me to mention your name if I

hear of any one wanting lodgings. I know there is no place where they could be half so comfortable."

Having said this he went out, and laughed to himself as he went back to the King's Arms. He was laughing at the idea of his recommending Mrs. Flint's lodgings, but perhaps the satisfaction he felt in the consciousness that Robert Ardwell was leaving Inverkeith that day week, may have had something to do with the heartiness of his merriment. The object which he had in view was accomplished without his interference, and although he had not the credit of doing a favour to his rival, he had not the risk of appearing to have cleared the way to his own success by a pseudo-favour to one whose presence he feared.

His opinion of Mrs. Flint was not high. He looked upon her as a sly, crafty woman,

who knew a great deal more than she
cared to show she knew, and who, while
she had succeeded in eliciting considerable
information from her questioner, had
communicated very little in return. Like
all men who only half understand human
nature, Sir John made a great mistake in
estimating her character, in ascribing all
her sorrow at parting with Mr. Ardwell
to the loss of a lodger who might not
count the lumps of sugar he left in the
sugar-basin, or measure his candle over
night, to see that it was not used during
the day. Only one thing is curious, and
that is, that Sir John in his dislike of Mr.
Ardwell did not ascribe these mean arti-
fices to him—but he could afford to be
generous. He had got Yetta's promise,
and Mr. Ardwell was going away.

CHAPTER XIII.

"Hearts, are like childrens' balls, and are oftenest caught in the recoil."

Wade.

IT is impossible to say whether Bernard Winn's verses were admirable or the reverse. He never showed them to Yetta, nor, what is more, to Frances Wardour, who might be supposed to be one of the persons who would have got a look at them, and that fact has some meaning; for, had the poem been written, Bernard would probably almost rather have shown it to Frances than to Yetta, as he knew that the former would have been unable to judge of its demerits, and would have praised the ingenuity which had got "love" to rhyme with "thereof," and, further, that if she had been able to gauge its contents, she would have praised it, because it came from him.

But not only did Frances never see the poem, she very seldom saw Bernard, and that seemed to her a worse calamity. She made 'every excuse for him. She used to hope that days which began in darkness would brighten, and that it might be fine weather for a month. She remembered that once Bernard used to be indifferent to showers, but she did not complain. It was sure to be fine weather soon. But even when the fine weather came, Bernard came but seldom. Once they nearly quarrelled a second time. Frances had been on High Cleugh, and Bernard was not there, so she wandered on until she came upon the Faldoon range of hills, and quite late in the afternoon she came upon Bernard, sitting on the hill-side, with

a book in his hand, and with his eyes
fixed upon some distant object in the
valley.

"Bernard," she said softly—Frances
laughed less now, and took Yetta for her
model.

"Oh, hang it, how you startled me!"
said Bernard, looking up, and he had
perhaps more colour in his face than the
occasion seemed to demand.

"I thought you meant to come to High
Cleugh to-day," she said.

"Did I? I forgot all about it. You
forget I have to work."

He was standing up now, and he
saw that Frances was holding out her
hand.

"Haven't I shaken hands with you?"
he said, and then he shook hands.

"Are you very busy?"

"Of course I am. I must earn my

bread. I am almost sorry I did not go back to school. It was all your doing that."

"I'll tell you what I've been thinking, Bernard."

"What is that? I dare say it's something very wise."

"I don't know whether it's wise or not, but I've been thinking that you don't care to walk with me now."

"Oh, are you at that again? I thought we had enough of that last time. But suppose I don't, for the sake of argument, what then?"

"Then I think with you, that it would have been much better if you had gone back to school."

"Now I'll tell you what, Frances. I wish you wouldn't come and bother me. Why can't you get Frank Maxwell or Charlie What's-his-name to walk with you? They have nothing to do, and I have."

"I will if you wish."

"I don't wish anything, except that you wouldn't come and trouble me when I'm busy."

"I won't come again, Bernard."

"Then don't," said Bernard, and he felt a mean pleasure in terminating the affair in that way.

But Frances could not look forward to a time when she would not see him at all; she would rather have him scold her every time, than not meet him. So she said,—

"Bernard, don't be angry. I didn't mean to bother you. But I came to-day because it is almost a whole week since I saw you. And I beg your pardon. But say you forgive me. Do!"

Bernard could not resist this entreaty, and the very sneaking pleasure which he had felt a moment ago at the prospect of quarrelling with Frances, and of which now he felt thoroughly ashamed, made him the more willing to forgive her for what was, after all, a very venial fault in his eyes; so he said kindly,—

"Well, don't cry. I was cross, and I didn't mean to be. You are a good little thing. I'll walk back with you."

And so he pocketed his book, and accompanied Frances almost the whole way to Kinskerth, and only got back to Faldoon when dinner was half over.

All this time Bernard was in the habit —like the pigeons when it is going to be stormy—of remaining close to home. He invariably smoked his pipe on the path which led past the stable and round by the tool-house in the fir-wood. Two days after that in which he had walked with Yetta, he was fortunate enough again to see Mary Gower. He saw her emerge from the wood, but instead of going to the stable-yard, in which her grandfather was working, she turned to the right and took the road which led round the garden. At first Bernard was disappointed, for he imagined that she turned off in that direction in order to avoid him. But self-conceit would not allow him to think so long, and the obvious inference from all the facts seemed to be that she had some other object for taking that road. Having begun by regretting this fact, he ended by rejoicing in it. And he determined to follow her, as he had no doubt he would find some opportunity of speaking to her. That was all he proposed to himself when he started. Mary Gower was unconscious that she was followed. She had not even seen Bernard, she knew that the road she was walking upon was always deserted after six o'clock, and as it was past seven, she felt that she was not in danger of being seen. Her own fear in that respect had passed away. She had been apprehensive that her grandfather might see her as she emerged from the wood, and it was her anxiety to avoid being seen by him that prevented her noticing Bernard. We move to avoid a swallow in its flight, and are struck down by a cannon-ball, which, but for our movement, would have passed us by on the other side. Bernard followed her at a considerable distance, but he did not follow her in a sneaking way. Had she looked back, she would have seen him; but she had too much to think of to guard against a pursuit of which she never dreamed. The road, when it reaches the tool-house in the fir-wood, turns towards the garden, but a foot-path runs from it and continues to ascend the hill in the cover of the wood, and it was this path that Mary Gower took.

This added infinitely to Bernard's wonder. He knew every part of the grounds about Faldoon, and he knew that that path led to no cottage or house, but up on to the bare hills. It was not the way which people were accustomed to use when they went up to the hills; that on the other side of the house, which led through the glen, being much better and easier of ascent. This circumstance excited his curiosity the more. Besides, it was past seven, and young women were not in the habit of clambering up these steep hills after the sun went down. Consequently Bernard reasoned that here was some mystery to which this conduct was a clue, and the idea of a mystery was delightful to him, especially when the person concerned in it was a beautiful girl. He thought that circumstances might occur which might even that very night give him an opportunity of being useful to her. There might be some villain to chastise—some—but his imagination of the ·possible peril was far inferior to his bold fancies of his own daring. However, as he went up the hill his speculations changed their complexion. He began to consider that the girl had probably gone to meet a lover, from whom she did not wish to be rescued, and the thought of it annoyed him. When he considered all the circumstances, he thought it must be a meeting sanctioned and approved by the young lady herself, and that it would be very improper of him to play the spy upon a lovers' meeting. So he retired into a little bosky shade, a short way off the path, for he was still anxious to see whether she came down alone, and there he sat down to wait.

It may have been half an hour that he sat there, and then he heard her footstep, and, peeping out, he saw that she was alone, but that she was weeping, and he sprang up and forced his way through the thicket to where she stood, as thoughts of revenge and rescue returned to his mind. She looked frightened at first, and then astonished, but she stood still, and waited till he should speak.

" I beg your pardon," said Bernard, " but I saw you were crying, and I thought I might help you. Has any one insulted you ? "

The question seemed ridiculous, but Mary Gower was not in a position to laugh at it, and her tears again flowed.

" I wish you would tell me," said Bernard ; " one doesn't cry for nothing, you know, and if I could be of use to you, I should so much like to. Won't you tell me?" he said earnestly.

"It would be of no use; no one would believe me," Mary said, and the necessity of thinking of the circumstances of her sorrow gave a fresh accession to her grief.

"I would believe you," said Bernard, "if all the world said it was a lie."

The girl looked up wonderingly to hear such words. She had ceased to cry, and she felt flattered, for she had only seen this boy once, and he said he would believe her if the world gave evidence against her! The assurance pleased her. She had just lost all hope of love from one person, who had assured her that, if she went to the world and told it of his promises, she would be regarded as mad, and laughed at. She had heard the same lips which used to press kisses and sweet whispers against her own, say that there was no love for her, and that he loved another. She felt a void in her life, and in her heart. Her high hopes lay low, and she wept for frustrated ambition as much as for lost love. At such a time the heart is open to impressions.

"I don't think you would believe me; he said nobody would. I have no proof. I have only my own word."

"I swear I will believe you," said Bernard impetuously. "It is lawyers and pettifoggers that require proof in writing, or proof by witnesses; but the word of an honest man or woman is better than all their written lies."

This was a somewhat unfair view of the subject, but it was generous, and Mary was convinced.

"It is very good of you, and if I told

any one, I would tell you, for you are very kind. But I don't think I shall tell any one, I shall try to bear it alone, I shall suffer without letting any one know why I grieve; but I did love him."

"Don't cry," said Bernard, and with a boldness which even, when he looked back upon it, astonished himself,—and yet the astonishment was not unaccompanied by a feeling of satisfaction,—he took her hand. "You can tell me or not, just as you please, but if any one has behaved badly to you, I should like to kick him. And if you did tell me all about it, it might be better, and I would promise not to tell any one."

He was actually stroking her hand!

"I cannot make up my mind whether I ought to tell you or not—at least, I cannot tell you now; it is getting dark; they will wonder where I have gone to."

" Well, but will you meet me here again to-morrow night, and then you can tell me if you like ? "

" I do not know whether I ought to come."

" Oh, yes, you ought," Bernard answered with a dogmatic certainty as to the ethical question, which was due to his failure to perceive one of the bearings of the act. " Do promise to come ! I will be here at seven, and wait for you. Will you promise ? "

" I might have made up my mind by that time, whether I should tell you," said Mary, giving an excellent reason for granting the request, which was as far away from the real reason as it was possible to be. But then she looked up with a half-smile in her eyes and said,—

" But you are so young."

" No, I am not. But, besides, what does

that matter? Pitt was Prime Minister at twenty-five, and Napoleon had done all sorts of extraordinary things before he was thirty. And I would do anything for you. At least, I would keep my word," he added, with an obscure consciousness that all the sorrow of this pretty girl was caused by falsity. "One does not need to be old to learn to keep one's promise."

"Well, let me go now. It is almost dark. Even now I will have to run the whole way."

She tried gently to disengage her hand, but Bernard held it fast and said,—

"Not till you promise."

They stood looking at each other for a few minutes, and then the girl said, smiling,—

"Well, I promise."

Bernard released her hand, and said good-night, and she hurried down the hill;

while he, feeling flushed and happy, went along the hill-side, and returned to the house by the way that led down the glen and over the foot-bridge.

CHAPTER XIV.

"Foul Jealousy! thou turnest love divine
  To joyless dread, and mak'st the loving heart
  With hateful thoughts to languish and to pine,
  And feed itself with self-consuming smart;
  Of all the passions in the mind, thou vilest art!"

Spenser.

SIR JOHN WARDOUR was not yet satisfied,
and that was not to be wondered at. He
could not make Yetta love him, and
although he was about to marry her
without her love, he hoped earnestly
that love would come, and he had such
self-reliance that he thought he could earn
it, and command it in time. His was a
character which had much of excellence
in it, mixed, fatally, with much baseness.

His main objects were noble, yet his subsidiary ends and means were often unworthy. There were veins of gold in the midst of much rubbishy earth. He generally worked and struck shafts into the latter, and neglected the former. However, Sir John had made up his mind to succeed in this matter, for he felt that Yetta's love would make his life nobler and better. He had studied her wishes, anticipated her wants, been gentle and kind, instead of clever and bitter, as was his wont. And none of these things had escaped Yetta's notice, and each was repaid with gratitude. But gratitude did not satisfy him; he wanted love. He perceived that she still thought of Robert Ardwell, for he saw her efforts to forget him. She never trusted herself alone. She seemed afraid of her own thoughts. She liked to be read to. She would start when she had been a little while silent, and begin to talk, as if there was some temptation to be avoided. She would listen to Mrs. Ramsay's gossip, and Mr. Newsome's heavy stories with avidity, almost as if she liked them.

All these things Sir John noted, and he thought he must find some other way of making her forget Robert Ardwell, than by simply allowing the crust of oblivion to settle slowly on her memory. If he could make her believe that Robert Ardwell was unworthy of her love, he thought he would have done much to attain his object. He set himself to find out something about the life of the young man, and that was by no means difficult to do. His friend Bainbridge, who had introduced Ardwell to him, must know something about him. So Bainbridge was written to, and he replied. The letter was partly satisfactory, but partly unsatisfactory. Everybody spoke highly of Mr. Ardwell. There was nothing in his life, so far as he knew, which would not bear the light of day, or any stronger light which might be thrown upon it. He was spoken of as a man of genius; he was eccentric, some of his relations admitted, but all agreed that his eccentricities were only exaggerations of virtue. All this was very unsatisfactory. But then followed some mention of a boyish love for a girl who had proved herself utterly unworthy of him, who had gone from bad to worse even during the time she was engaged to Robert Ardwell, and now was sunk so low as to be unworthy of the name of woman. Mr. Ardwell's engagement had been broken off years before, and yet it was said that he gave up the whole of his annual income, which he had under his father's will, to enable the

woman to live honestly, and that, although
it was ample, and he lived, for the want of
it, in comparative poverty himself, it had
not the desired effect. This seemed to
Sir John somewhat satisfactory, and the
day after that on which he received this
letter, he went over to Faldoon to tell
Yetta that he had to go to England for
a few days on business. Yetta used
some polite words of courtesy, and he
said,—

"Yetta, tell me, do you care whether I
go or stay? Does my presence bring you
no light? Would you rather that I did
not come?"

"No, I am very grateful to you for
coming. Your presence seems to help me,
and you are so kind and good, and are never
tired of reading to me, and you talk so well.
Your intelligence seems to cleave like a
scimitar to the heart of things. I like to

listen ; it helps me so much. I am sorry
you have to go."

He did not ask her how his presence helped her, for he knew ; but he
said,—

"Will you love me in time, Yetta ?"

And she answered,—

"I will try."

So he went away.

It was late autumn now. The mornings
came bright, but crystallized, like sugared
fruit. The afternoon fell into early evenings and the night came quick with black,
dull sky. Each end of the day was sharp
with prickles of frost, and people in rooms
migrated from the window to the fireside.
The window-panes were covered with
spirit-drawings of the frost, and everything told of a summer gone, and of a
winter, with its reign of terror, come.
Still, these short, bright days were pleasant,

and although they did not permit of loitering, they encouraged the enjoyment of motion, and Yetta had always a ready guide in Bernard. The day after Sir John had gone, Bernard led Yetta along the highroad which leads towards Kinskerth. When they came to a pretty piece of roadway, or a place where the country is spread like some great peacock's tail to those who have clambered up the hill, while to those who are on the plain all its eyes are hidden, he would stop, and try to describe the view to her. He had not much power of description, but the sense that they were there before her, although she could not see them, enabled her to think vividly of the scenes they passed by. When they were on the hill which overlooks the Kinskerth valley, Bernard said suddenly,—

"By the way, Yetta, are you very fond of Sir John?"

"Why do you ask, Bernard?" Yetta said gently.

"I don't know, but I was thinking that one ought not to marry, unless one was very fond of one's husband or wife."

"Perhaps not, Bernard, but one must not break a promise."

"No, that's what I say, hang it!"

After this somewhat inconsequential answer Bernard was silent, and they continued their walk.

"When will Sir John be back, Yetta?"

"I don't know; he seemed uncertain. Why?"

"I want to have a talk with him, that's all," said Bernard with an important air.

CHAPTER XV.

"Thou wilt stick at nothing. What! would you lie
to secure her love? Methinks, before thou hast gotten
her affection, she will have discovered thy trick, and
reward thee with contempt and hatred."

The Disturbed Dovecot.

Sir John returned in the course of a few
days, and drove over to Faldoon soon
after his arrival.

It was a cold, bright day, but not too
cold to drive out, and as Yetta always
assented to whatever he proposed, she
went to prepare for a drive, while Sir
John talked to Mrs. Graham.

"How is Yetta?" asked Sir John.

"She is very well," answered Mrs. Graham, who cherished the same belief as Sir

John, that time must inevitably make her daughter love the strong, handsome man that stood before her. "And I think," she added, "that she is almost more cheerful than she used to be."

"I am glad of that. I mean to ask her to tell me when we may be married, if I have your approval."

"Of course you have, Sir John."

"I hear there is some chance of a dissolution, and she would begin to take an interest in my canvass, and that would do her good. She wants to lead a more active life. Faldoon is very pleasant, but it is very quiet. It would do her good to go to town for a season, and receive lots of visitors. Of course, Frances could help her."

"I'm sure it would be delightful."

"I don't know whether you have noticed, Mrs. Graham, that my sister Frances is

ever so much improved by her associa-
tion with Yetta; she used to be a laughing, romping hoyden, and now she is
quiet and gentle; Yetta has done her all
the good in the world."

At that moment Yetta came to the
door and said, "I am ready;" and Sir
John went out into the hall, and as he
was putting on Yetta's fur, he could not
resist the temptation of kissing her.
He was evidently happier than usual that
day.

"Do you know, Yetta," Sir John said,
as he drove towards Inverkeith, "I hear
that there will probably be a dissolution in
a few months, and I want you to help
me in the election; but you could not
do that at Faldoon, you must come to
Kinskerth as my wife."

"Oh no, please, not yet. It is too
soon; I could not, could not."

Her voice was very earnest, and full of entreaty.

"Why not, Yetta? Your mother was just saying that if you took an interest in the election it would do you good. You lead too quiet a life at Faldoon."

"I shall take an interest in anything you wish. I will go and canvass for you, I will do anything, but please do not ask me to marry you for a long time yet."

"I don't want you to be interested because I tell you to be. I don't want to make a slave of you, Yetta, but I want you to take an interest in it because it interests me."

"So I will, so I am. I am not so utterly callous. I am interested in your ambition. I should be selfish if I were not moved by what moves you; you are always so kind and good—too kind, too good.

But do not make me marry you for a time, not for a long time yet."

" I don't want to make you marry me, but my ambition is only a little part of my love ; and if the former throbs in you, why cannot the latter, too ? "

" I don't know, but I do try."

" Yetta," he said in a low, deep voice, which was almost lost in the noise of the wheels, " do you still care for Robert Ardwell ? "

There was a pause, and then Yetta answered, as if despairingly,—

" I am afraid I do."

" Would you still care for him, if you found him unworthy, capable of baseness, of cruelty ? "

" I don't know, but that is impossible."

She spoke calmly.

" But what if I told you that he is not

what you think him—that he had loved
and promised to marry another woman,
that she had trusted him too much, that
he deserted her, and that then she sank
lower and lower without a helping hand
from him, although he was conscious that
he was the cause of her degradation."

"I would not believe you."

"Well, I tell you that it is true."

"And I tell you it is false," cried Yetta,
and her sightless eyes flashed upon him,
and her lip quivered; "and I tell you
more," she added, "that it is not the
way to win love to breathe calumny against
another; it is mean and base, and unworthy
of you. I did not think you would stoop
so low."

"You will be sorry for this, Yetta."

"No, I shall not be sorry," she said
proudly, "for defending the innocent
against vile lies."

"Then you will not give credence to what I say?"

"No, not against him. You have some object; I don't know, and would rather not guess, what it is. But you hate him, and this is your mean revenge. Duelling was better than backbiting."

She spoke rapidly, with a clear, nervous utterance, and her cheeks were sometimes as white as snow, and sometimes as pink as a rosebud.

"Listen to me, Yetta. You behave like a child. You are noble, I dare say, but still childish. What I hinted at is too true. Surely proof is somewhat stronger than your instinct. Surely the woman he wronged and deserted must know more than you do. Surely those who have suffered want and misery through his inhuman cruelty are better able to judge of his nobility of soul, his generosity of heart, and uprightness of character, than you who have heard him play once or twice on the organ or the piano, and may have had an interesting conversation on the fingering of a piece of music, or on the peculiarities of the chromatic scale."

" I do not believe it," said Yetta in a low voice ; " I know more of him than that. Some instincts may be false, mine cannot be."

" Well, if you go in for omniscience, I have nothing more to say. Only I shall be glad when you come to your senses, that you should apologize to me for having doubted my truth. Your instincts may be infallible, but as I had no such guide to go by, I felt constrained to believe what was proved by incontrovertible evidence."

" And if it is true," said Yetta, with a bitter smile, " you were good enough to take the trouble to find it out and to tell me."

"It was partly forced upon me, and I thought it better that you should know the truth than believe a lie. That was my reason for telling you."

"I feel cold," said Yetta; "I should like to go home now."

Sir John turned the ponies' heads, and drove quickly back through the keen air towards Inverkeith, through its rough, stony streets, and then towards Faldoon. During the whole of the drive Yetta never spoke, and when she reached home, she went at once to her own room. It was harder to bear this than to bear all else beside.

Meanwhile Mrs. Graham came to the door, and pressed Sir John to remain to dinner.

"Thank you, I must not stay to-day. After one's return home there is always a good deal to do. I have letters to write."

" And did Yetta give you a decided answer, Sir John? It must be her own doing, for I have little or no influence with her now."

" No, Yetta was very unreasonable to-day. . We quarrelled."

" Dear me, I'm very sorry! I dare say she will be grieved about it to-morrow, or even by dinner-time, for she is never angry long. I wish you would stay. Besides, I heard Bernard say he wanted to speak with you."

" Thank you. I must not remain to-day. And as for Bernard, tell him to come to lunch to-morrow. I will come back to Faldoon when I am sent for."

Mrs. Graham was very much distressed. It occurred to her mind that Sir John might wish to be released from his engagement in consequence of this quarrel, and that would have been a dire calamity in her estimation. She thought that Sir John's position, estates, and income were in every way desirable, and that the possibility of its being bruited abroad that Sir John had broken off his engagement with Miss Graham on account of her bad temper, would prevent other eligible suitors from coming forward. And, besides, she was not insensible to the disadvantage Yetta laboured under, looked at in a matrimonial point of view, from being blind. Of course she knew that the possessor of Faldoon would not be without offers, but ever since Yetta's good fortune had been made known to her, Mrs. Graham's one intense fear had been that she might fall a prey to some needy adventurer, who married her for her fortune.

All her motherly instincts repelled her

powerfully from such a horrible thought, and it was this possible anticipation which made her the more strenuously support the cause of Sir John, who was certainly above the suspicion of wishing to marry Yetta for her money. These considerations made her look upon the quarrel as a real calamity, and she determined that nothing she could do to bring about a reconciliation should be left undone.

Almost immediately after Sir John had driven away, Mrs. Graham went upstairs and knocked at the door of Yetta's room. At first there was no answer, so she knocked again. Then she heard Yetta say, " Wait a minute," and in a few moments Yetta opened the door, and Mrs. Graham saw that she had been weeping.

" What is the matter?" asked her

mother as she went in and led Yetta to a low chair by the fire. "You have been crying."

"Yes, I have; something has occurred which vexes me."

"I'm glad to hear you say that, Yetta. I knew you wouldn't bear ill-feeling, and it shows you are sorry for having quarrelled, already."

"It is not *that* I am sorry for," said Yetta, raising her head proudly. "Has he been complaining to you?"

"Complaining? nothing of the sort! Only he seemed hurt, and I asked him to stay to dinner, and then he said he should not come to Faldoon again, until he was wanted. He was quite polite," added Mrs. Graham, feeling that her report of the interview she had had with Sir John was perhaps calculated to leave a false impression upon Yetta's mind.

"Oh, I have no doubt he was polite, that is his forte. It is wonderful what inferior substances take a superior polish."

"I wish you would not talk in that way, Yetta. If you mean to say that Sir John is an ungenerous man, I must say I don't agree with you. And as for politeness, I like it. I wouldn't like to be called a liar to my face, even if a person thought it. But tell me, Yetta, what is it that vexes you?"

"Oh! there is no use talking about it, mamma; you would be sure to take Sir John's part, and say I had done wrong and been rude; but I'm glad I was rude. I wish I had said something else that it was in my head to say, and I would have cut him to the quick."

"Yetta! Yetta! I never saw you like this before."

"You never saw me after I had had to

sit and hear a friend slandered by one whom I have promised to marry. Oh, that I had never given that promise! You never saw me after I had heard what would make me more miserable than death if I believed it, and that from one who, professing to love me, had taken the trouble to root out the foul story, thinking I would be interested doubtless in the vile romance."

"Yetta, calm yourself. This looks more like insanity than anything else. Do talk reasonably, and tell me what Sir John said."

"Oh! it is no use going over it again. I heard enough of it, and yet, had I given him a little encouragement, he would have enlarged on it—and that is love!"

"You know very well, Yetta, that Sir John is devoted to you. I have heard you say so, and it isn't fair, just because of some little lovers' quarrel, to go and say that he doesn't love you, when you know he does."

"A lovers' quarrel! If lovers quarrel as we did, I pity their love. I did believe he loved me. Even now I dare say he thinks he loves me. But I did not give him credit for so coarse a nature. He mistakes me, if he thinks to win me by such arts."

"What does it all mean, Yetta? You go rambling on, forgetting that I know nothing about it; and if, as you say, you do not wish to tell me, because you believe I would take Sir John's side, then I say the chances are you were in the wrong, and the best thing you can do is to ask his forgiveness."

"Ask his forgiveness! I would not ask his pardon for a single word I said; I only regret that I didn't say more."

"Yetta, this is very unchristian, very

unlike you. You have generally a most feeling heart, and you would have been sorry if you had seen how hurt he was."

" I do feel, I can feel, but it is for the injured, not for the destroyer. I can feel for the innocent, not for the guilty. I have no feeling for Sir John."

Mrs. Graham was utterly astonished. She had never heard Yetta speak in this way before. All Yetta's past had been quiet and calm and gentle, but now she was shaken by a fierce storm. In times past she had wept her anger away, and then asked forgiveness, although she had done no wrong. She was always nervously sensitive for others. Sympathy was her nervous system. But now she seemed to disregard Sir John Wardour, whose least word until that day had been a command, and regretted that she had not inflicted some deeper injury upon him.

All these strange phenomena puzzled and confused Mrs. Graham. She thought at one minute of sending for Dr. Arbwith, at another for the clergyman, but after considering for some time she decided that the best way was to leave Yetta to herself —and she was right.

One can scarcely trace all the roots of one's emotions. Yetta's anger was partly self-defence against an idea which would force itself upon her. He had said he could prove all he had said. It was that thought that tormented her. If she had been told it was all a lie, if she had been assured that there was no truth in any word Sir John had said, she could have forgiven him at once, and would scarcely have felt any anger. But it was the growing consciousness that it might be true; that, after all, her instinct of love, which she thought a touch-stone of character might not

tell true; that inexorable facts might
prove this man unworthy and despicable—
it was that thought that gave her agony,
and it was to avoid it, that she indulged
her anger against Sir John. She felt that
the more she could despise him, the less
likely was she to believe his assertion.
But when she was alone, his horrible words
came back to her. Had she ever known
him guilty of a lie? Were not witnesses
more to be relied on than instincts? Could
he prove it?

The dinner-gong sounded, but she did
not hear it. The light faded, but she did
not know it. Bernard came and knocked
at her door, and asked if he should bring
her some tea, but she answered, "No,
thank you."

She still lay upon her bed, with her face
buried in the pillows, when her mother
knocked at the door to say "Good-night."

And long into the night she lay there, tormenting herself with that thought, until, tired with excitement and with weeping, she fell asleep.

CHAPTER XVI.

" Ah, your glass and you are colleagued, to turn your silly head inside out. But for shame I would break the compact, for the head is an empty one."

Bain.

To be made a confidant is infinitely pleasant, but to be made the confidant of a very pretty girl in a quiet distant wood, in the silent evening hours, while the west is yellow with the trail of the day, must be even more so, and Bernard Winn felt that he was one of the luckiest of men, and that, up to the present time, Mary Gower had been one of the most unlucky of women. He returned from that interview on the hill-side, through the springing shades of the evening, very much in love with the pretty girl who had told him all her secret, and very angry with certain other persons who were more or less directly connected with the sorrowful secret of which he was the custodian. His feelings might have been somewhat accurately determined by those who had heard him say snappishly, in answer to Yetta's question why he never went to Kinskerth now,—

"Oh! I can't be bothered. It is no fun. Miss Wardour is ridiculous with her Utopian ideas, and wearies one's life out by insisting upon my taking an interest in sanitary reform, and all that sort of humbug. And Frances is a hoyden, and seems to have come into the world to giggle."

Yetta said nothing in answer to this peppery little diatribe, but when next she saw Frances, she was kinder to her than she had been before, and the girl felt it, and laid her head on Yetta's lap and wept.

Meanwhile Mary Gower had gone home, and had looked at herself in the glass, and thought what a blank life Yetta Graham's must'be, without the possibility of indulging in that luxury. The result of that inspection seemed to satisfy her, for she smiled, and the two little dimples dawned in her cheeks, as the planet of love might peep out of a rosy heaven. She was wondering what Bernard Winn had thought of her, and perhaps she came to a correct conclusion, when she said,—

"I think he must have thought me pretty. His eyes were full of admiration."

At that instant her grandfather came into the room, and said,—

"Weel, Mary, are ye keekin' at yersel'

in the glass? Ye are unco' vain, I'm thinkin', and ye weel may be, for ye're a bonnie lass; but, mind ye, the lilies of the field were better dressed than Solomon, and although they are sae beautiful, they dinna haud their heads so high."

James Milligan's lectures to his granddaughter were somewhat anomalous, for while he enunciated the highest principles of conduct, he seemed to hint that if these were not followed out by Mary, every excuse was to be made for her. He had a Spartan code, with a Christian way of dispensing it, and that, in the case of Mary, tended to become rather lax. He generally terminated his lectures, as he did upon this occasion, with the censure, "I fear ye are a light-headed creature," the severity of which was considerably modified by the tone in which it was uttered.

Mrs. Gower entered the room, as usual intent upon some domestic matter.

"Well, Mary," she said, "are you in better spirits? One would think you were sorry to come home; you must find this dull after Edinburgh."

"No, I don't, mother; but I have had something to vex me."

"Nonsense, Mary! What troubles can you have? You don't know you are in existence yet."

"Oh, yes, I do, mother," said Mary, with some sadness in her voice, but she was not one of those persons who suffer deeply, and soon she smiled again.

"I was hearing to-day that Miss Graham's marriage is fixed for early spring," said Mrs. Gower, "but it may be nonsense."

"I hope she'll be happy when she does marry," said Mary bitterly.

" What do you mean, Mary ? "

"I mean, mother, that I don't think she will be happy, that's all."

"Not happy ? I would like to know who should be happy, if not she ? She has everything to make her happy, and I'll warrant she has a clear conscience."

" Oh, I don't know anything about *her*."

" Well, and what do you know against Sir John ? "

" Oh, I know—I know a good deal. Everybody said he was tyrannical in turning that poor man out of the High Cleugh farm, and that shows he has no heart."

" Well, I never ! You stood up for Sir John through thick and through thin, and wouldn't hear a word said against him when Mr. Flint was here and said it was tyrannical ; and now, forsooth, you say he has no heart! You are as changeable as a weathercock, Mary."

"I know more now," said Mary.

"Have they made ye a Radical in Edinbro', woman?" asked her grandfather, who had been listening to the conversation, as he picked up the cinders on the hearth with the tongs. He used formerly to use his fingers for the same purpose, on the ground of their priority in the order of creation, but now he used the tongs, to please Mary.

"No, I don't know anything about politics, and don't want to," said Mary; "but I think Sir John is a bad man."

"We are nane o' us sae gude as we ought to be, Mary," put in the old man, "and I dare say Sir John has his faults."

"Oh, yes," said the girl, "there is something bad in his face."

"Well, Mary, you have changed your

mind about that, for you used to think Sir John's face perfect, and I remember you asking me if I had ever seen a handsomer man."

"He is handsome, but there is something wicked in his face. I know there is. I think Mr. Winn is better-looking. He has such a good face, and I'm sure he's kind, and wouldn't turn a man out of his farm, if he had one, and wouldn't do lots of other things."

It was evident from this and other utterances of Mary's, that Bernard had made a favourable impression upon her, and that for some reason her good opinion of his character stood out in relief from her bad opinion of Sir John. That night, when she went to bed, Mary took off the ruby ring from her finger, and laid it away in a drawer which she locked. It had never been off her finger since she got it until now. Then she knelt down, and said her prayers; then she gave a last look in the glass, before she extinguished the light, and crept into bed.

END OF VOL. II.

GILBERT AND RIVINGTON, LIMITED ST. JOHN'S SQUARE, LONDON.

www.ingramcontent.com/pod-product-compliance
Lightning Source LLC
Chambersburg PA
CBHW031423020726
47499CB00005B/1565